BLOOD DRIVE

A Vampire / Otherkin Novel

by

TRACI HOUSTON

EDITED BY COREY MICHAEL BLAKE

Copyright © 2011 Traci Houston
Writers of the Round Table Press

ISBN Paperback: 978-1-61066-009-9

Library of Congress Control Number: 2011934100

Published By:
Writers of the Round Table Press
1670 Valencia Way
Mundelein, IL 60060
Phone: 224.475.0392
www.roundtablecompanies.com
www.blooddrivebook.com

Cover Design and Interior Layout by:
Nathan Brown, Round Table Companies

Thanks to Sam and Laurell Houston, mom and dad, for telling me I could be anything I wanted to be, and meaning it. To my daughter, Laurell, for cooking dinner so I could write. To my daughter, Tricia, for the tech support and keeping my laptop from exploding.

INTRODUCTION

The blood was still on Cara's hands. She had washed them everyday, all day, for the last week but she could swear that her partner's blood—warm and wet—still clung to her fingertips. She had done everything by the book, knew in her heart that she could not have saved him, but every morning the blood was still there and every night it replayed in her dreams while this hunk of metal burned in her pocket. She had kept it with her not knowing why, she simply knew it was important to keep it and keep it hidden. As she moved around her apartment preparing herself for her coming interview she wished for Danny's voice telling her it was okay, that everything was fine, but that voice was dead and she couldn't shake the feeling that she'd killed it.

CHAPTER 1

Cara Evens walked quickly down the central corridor of the Miami Police department, idly taking note of the officers who ran their eyes over her. They watched the petite, black-haired beauty from a careful distance, but dared not approach her. Cara was thankful they gave her plenty of space. She'd worked for the past week to strengthen her ability to block out the emotions people seemed to spill all over her. Unfortunately for her, the closer people got to her the harder she had to work at keeping their feelings from having an effect on her. It certainly wasn't her looks that held them back, or her smooth, tanned skin, or even the black curls that, for the first time in her recollection, hung just past her shoulders. Sometimes she allowed her eyes to meet their own full on, only to watch their gazes slide quickly away. Cara was but five feet five inches and lean, but she was deceptively powerful. The men who now held themselves back were not physically intimidated, although some of them should have been.

No, what held them back was her partner's death. She had been alone with Danny Brooks on the job when he had died. They had stood by her through the funeral and services because she was one of them, but now the mourning period was over and doubts were setting in. Some of them were recalling what she looked like with her partner's blood staining her hands. She could almost read the questions in their gazes: If Danny's partner had been a man, would he still be alive? Could a man have been physically faster, mentally quicker; aware enough to know that something was off?

Danny had been a cop's cop. His broad shoulders and solid build made up for the "boy next door" looks. White blond hair and gray eyes increased his popularity with the ladies and gave Cara plenty of teasing ammunition. He bled blue, and he had stepped up for Cara the first time she had been subjected to questioning looks. After all, she was a woman in a largely man's world. For that, and a hundred more facts like that, he'd been her cop, her friend, her backup.

Glancing at her watch, she saw that she was twenty minutes early for her appointment with the new captain. Although she had known Captain Monahan since birth, this was the first time she would be under his command. She had made detective.

Turning left at the end of the hall, she ducked into the women's rest room. Inspecting her reflection, she questioned herself for the thousandth time. Staring herself hard in the eye, she mentally turned back the clock one week...

Cara sat in the passenger seat of the parked patrol car snatching bites of a cheeseburger while her partner, Danny Brooks, checked his list of things he needed to accomplish in the next week.

"I need an assistant." Danny frowned at his list.

"You can't have that much to do." Cara glanced at him while trying to keep all the ketchup on her burger.

"Get my dress blues dry cleaned, buy new shoes, and get a haircut. I also have to finish shopping for the party. You do remember the party I'm giving after the ceremony?"

"You remind me every seven seconds. Shoes? Hair? Party? Are you sure you're not a woman?" Cara eyed him suspiciously then burst out laughing.

Danny's indignant expression melted into a sheepish grin. "It's good to hear you laugh again, Evens. You've been stressing way too much about this detective thing."

Cara's laughter dissolved, and she wiped her eyes. She took another bite of her cheeseburger, delaying her response. Danny knew her well enough to know that the promotion bothered her, but long ago Cara developed the talent of keeping her emotions locked safely behind a wall.

She finished chewing, swallowed, then took a measured breath and continued, "I just don't want to get *those* looks. The ones that ask whether I was promoted to fill the girl quota."

"You've got a perfect record. *We* were promoted on merit, thank you very much. Next week we will be given our detective badges and be out of these uniforms. You're not going to get any looks."

Danny watched as the future and all its possibilities ran through her mind. He knew that under her police cap was a tight bun that, once undone, would spill blue-black curly hair past her shoulders. It would surround a heart-shaped face that sported almond-shaped green eyes that tilted up ever so slightly at the corners. Her small pert nose and full lips could nearly have a guy believing in fairies. His partner worked out religiously and made sure that power was packed into every shapely inch. He had been grateful for that power and the agility that accompanied it in more than one tight spot that they had gotten into. She was deceptively feminine. Danny thought that it worked to her advantage, but Cara thought it caused more problems than not.

Dispatch broke into his thoughts; the sterile voice alerting them to a silent alarm only two blocks away. Danny hit the accelerator while Cara wrapped their burgers and fries back into their foil envelopes with one hand while reaching for the radio to respond with the other. He was glad it was late. Danny loved the element of surprise and empty streets allowed them to drive without flashing lights or wailing sirens.

Danny pulled the patrol car over to the curb one building away from where the alarm had gone off and together they left the car without a sound. The one-story building they headed towards could have been any color. The street lights were dim, making the alleys on either side of it ominous. Moving to the positions enacted countless times, Cara waited at the front for Danny to take his place at the back and give her the signal to move in. She glanced at the sign on the front of the building and relaxed slightly; a blood bank. Some employee probably left something behind and forgot the place was wired.

The blinds on the front door were pulled, obscuring her view of the inside. Suddenly her body tingled with apprehension: it was wrong, the whole thing was wrong! Throwing aside the code of absolute silence, she sprinted toward the alley Danny had disappeared into, turning the corner, and flying with every ounce of energy she possessed down the darkened corridor. A scream tore through the night air and Cara stumbled as if she'd been shot. That was not the signal she'd been waiting for.

Regaining her balance, she reached the back street but saw no sign of Danny. Pausing only long enough to call for backup through the radio attached to her shoulder, she headed straight to the back entrance. The door stood open and light from the building behind her dimly revealed the way inside. Somehow assured that any assailants had fled, she pulled the flashlight from her belt and made her way in.

Instantly she knew that this had been no employee returning for a forgotten set of car keys. Refrigerators and freezers stood open. Blood and glass lay everywhere. Sensing more than seeing, she turned the flashlight to the left. A blue uniformed body with white-blond hair lay on the floor, resembling a rag doll tossed in the corner. Cara made a rapid survey of the rest of the building and returned to the body within seconds, knowing it was Danny's. She hoped that most of the blood surrounding him came from the vandalized blood supplies, and not from any wound he had suffered. The wail of sirens split the air as Cara reached down to take Danny's pulse.

As her fingers sank into the flesh of his neck, she refused to accept what she felt. His throat had been slashed from ear to ear. There was no saving him. Everything froze and a vision grabbed her. In her mind, she saw Danny come through the back door and she fought the urge to yell out and warn him. A figure whirled out of the darkness and attacked. Warm blood ran over her fingers where she had probed for a sign of life, and just as suddenly everything came back into focus again. Danny was dead. She pulled her hand away and then felt it, a something that called to her. Cara reached over Danny's body and her hand closed around an object without looking at it. She was breaking a number of rules pounded into her as a police officer, but she knew this was for her and her alone. Still not sparing it a glance she shoved it in her pocket as backup arrived.

Over and over she made her report to the officers answering the call for backup, to the homicide detectives arriving on the scene, and to the captain who showed up because one of his men was down in the line of duty. To Cara, it seemed as if every officer on the Miami police force personally requested her to file her report that evening. She could feel the grief welling up. Each time she shoved it back down. The captain told her to take a week off and another officer drove her home.

The muffled sound of a door opening behind her drew Cara back to the present. It was time to face the captain. He had requested she report to his office, no doubt to give her some desk work sure to drive her batty. Dawson and Ross were investigating Danny's death. She knew there was no way she could get near the case and that burned her.

Continuing down the hallway she turned into the detectives' bull pen. Making right for the captain's office she rapped twice gently, but distinctly on his door. A voice inside called out a terse, "Come in!" and Cara turned the handle and entered.

Cara eyed Captain Monahan's calm face. Hair that had once been black was now salt and pepper. He was still impressive sitting behind his desk. The hours he spent at the gym made his uniform fit to perfection. Even though his square face had acquired its fair share of lines, his eyes were sharp and as far as Cara knew, had never missed a trick.

Those steel grey eyes swept over her now and she knew he was evaluating what he saw.

"Sit. Got a little something I need you to take care of." Captain Monahan slid the file across the desk and waited for Cara to open it. Silence settled over the room as she read her former partner's name on the label.

Cara looked to the Captain, her eyes asking the question.

"Couple of interviews that didn't get taken care of yet. Watterson, Thomas; his information as a contact wasn't on file. The information we had was of his predecessor. We've gotten in touch with him, and he's expecting you. Iverly, Jonathan; out of the country. He should be arriving today. These are the *only* aspects of this particular investigation you are to be involved with. Are we clear?" Cara calculated just how many strings he had pulled to get this done. Lots and lots.

He reached across the desk for the file. "Well, if you don't think you can handle it—"

"I can handle it." She snatched the file out of his reach, her voice defiant, but her eyes showing gratitude.

"Then get your ass out of my office."

Cara reached her desk just as Paul Vinton did. Vinton only topped her by a few inches, and his long thin face brought to mind a ferret. Cara had never cared for him. He thought having a badge meant he didn't have to answer for any of his actions. She kept her eyes averted, hoping that if she ignored him she could avoid a conflict. No such luck.

"I don't see any partner tagging along. Were they afraid you might lose another one?"

Cara wanted to punch him until all of his teeth fell out of his head, and she might have if she hadn't glanced over his shoulder. Instead, her face broke out into a terrific smile. Vinton's sneer turned to confusion. He was not used to people smiling at him, particularly females. He realized that Cara's eyes were focused not on him but on something, or someone, over his right shoulder. He turned to see what attracted her attention and saw Mason Havilland approaching. Vinton took the opportunity to make a hasty retreat.

"I think you scared him away," Cara continued to grin at Mason.

"I hope so. He almost blew the Dizzazio case. Ramos came close to taking him apart. I think he'll be staying away from my team for a while." She knew that Mason had liked her the minute she had walked through the department doors. One session of hand-to-hand in the gym had cured his misconception that she was too small to take care of herself and had done much to pique his interest. He was also six foot five, so she supposed that small was relative to him.

"Still trying to rid the world of organized crime?" Mason was her harmless flirtation. He was built like a brick house, but his heart was pure teddy bear, as long as you weren't a criminal. She had fun with the easy banter.

"Dawson and Ross are good detectives. They'll get him." Mason's voice lowered and softened on the last couple of syllables.

"They'd better."

She watched his eyes widen in shock when her tone went flat and hard. "Look, I'm sorry, I have to go." She fled. She could feel it. It was coming.

CHAPTER 2

Cara rushed to her car, squealed out of the parking lot, and pulled into an empty alley. Cutting the engine, she watched her hands shaking. A kaleidoscope of feelings flooded her; despair, anger, hate, grief—every emotion she had suppressed for the past two weeks surfaced with a vengeance. Her knuckles turned white as she gripped the wheel. After five minutes the shakes reduced to a few shudders, leaving her face flushed. *What the hell? Never during the day, never.* This was the price she paid for her ability to hide and control every emotion. A dull ache settled behind her eyes. Turning on the car and putting the air on full blast, Cara began repairing her light make-up. She didn't want to analyze her reaction again. Cara had already dismissed her reaction to Danny's death. Psychic abilities were no longer a part of her life. The vision she put off as an aberration of extreme emotional stress and the empathy was already fading. The emotions of others were down to barely a wisp. She had no time for past tragedies; she could only deal with the present one. She was just thankful no one had witnessed her overload. Taking one final look into the mirror at her face, she was confident that she was once more in complete control as she pulled into traffic.

She parked her car in almost the same spot that she and Danny had parked a week ago. Sitting inside the car, she scanned the building. It certainly had a different feel to it in broad daylight. Cara took the file Monahan had given her on Danny's investigation out of her briefcase and flipped through it. Her mouth dropped open as she realized that not only was the information for her two assigned interviews there, but also most of the information that had been collected thus far by the other detectives. Monahan had made sure she had copies of everything. She exhaled and silently thanked him. She stopped at the autopsy report, knowing the crime scene and autopsy pictures lay behind it. She wouldn't look at them now.

She left the car and entered the building, this time through the front door. The place was spotless.

"Is there something I can help you with?" the receptionist behind the desk asked.

Cara flashed her badge and replied, "Detective Cara Evens from the Miami Police department. I need to speak to Thomas Watterson." The receptionist's smile dimmed and Cara mentally noted it.

"I guess you're looking for me."

Cara was startled as a man spoke from behind her. She could usually sense someone before she saw them, no matter how quietly they walked, but this voice had come from nowhere. Cara turned, took a casual step back, and eyed the man behind the voice. Nothing remarkable: five foot ten, two hundred pounds, reddish brown hair, brown eyes, and a solid build. Summarizing people into mug shots was a useful habit of hers. She went back to his eyes.

Again Cara stated her business, and in return was shown to his office.

"I guess we get a real detective this time because an officer was killed?" Cara hadn't been there two minutes, and she could sense he already wanted her gone.

"The officer who was killed was my partner. He was killed protecting *your* place of business."

"I'm sorry, the last time this happened we got no cooperation from the police. An officer came down, we signed a complaint, and that was it." Thomas took a cleansing breath. "Look, why don't we start over. I'm Thomas Watterson, director of operations for the center." He reached across the desk for her hand.

"Detective Evens." She shook his hand, but her tone said, *not forgiven.* "I will need to ask you and some of your employees a few questions." His eyes were so blank. "You mentioned other problems. Any reason to believe they are related?"

"I don't know. It was a year ago, but it's possible."

"What about the employees here?"

"I seriously doubt that anyone here is capable of murder."

"Keep in mind that the death was not premeditated," she reminded him. "Until the confrontation ensued, I'm sure that death was not the goal here."

"True. Let me rephrase that statement then. I don't think anyone here has any reason to harm the center. Most of them have been here since we opened."

"Who has been hired recently?"

"Only Miriam. I am positive it wasn't her."

"For what reason?"

"She's 63. Even though she's in good shape for a 63-year-old woman, I don't think she could have taken a man the size and strength of your partner."

Cara sensed his patience slipping. "How do you know my partner's size?"

"The white outline the police left. I realize it's not accurate, but he still had to be a pretty big guy. Besides, policemen in general tend to be better prepared for hand-to-hand combat than women preparing to retire."

"Where were you that night?"

"A fund-raiser. I was one of the speakers that night."

"What time did you speak?"

"We had dinner at about eight, and I was the fourth speaker. I'd say I got behind the pulpit around nine, and then there was entertainment later. I took a few people home, we had the company limo. I said goodnight to my doorman about twelve-thirty."

"You seem to have accounted for your time very well."

"It's my job to keep track of my time."

"Have you let anyone go lately? The person Miriam replaced?"

"Miriam was an addition."

"Anyone outside the clinic that might want to do it harm?" She already knew what the answer was going to be.

"No."

"Who funds the center?" Nothing showed in this man's eyes. Even when his voice dripped with sarcasm.

"Iverly holdings. They fund many charities and community centers in the area. In fact, it was their fundraiser I attended that night."

"I'd like to take a look at the employee records, as well as your files of people who have donated or received blood in the recent past."

"All of those records were destroyed that night. Copies are kept at the main office." He handed her a business card. "You won't be able to see those files without Mr. Iverly's permission, unless you have a warrant, or whatever it is you get to paw through people's things."

"Never heard it put like that, but I will certainly make sure I go through proper channels before I start pawing." *This guy is something else.* "I would like to speak to the employees today if possible." She didn't take her eyes off of him.

"Why? Expect one of them to confess?"

"At this point I don't suspect any of your employees. All I want to know right now is if they have seen anyone spending more time here than they should, or if anyone is harassing them in their personal lives."

With that, she decided that the interview was over. She didn't wait for his permission or even his acknowledgment; she simply stood up and left his office. She'd hoped the employee files would be here.

Thoughtfully Cara tapped Jonathan Iverly's business card against her palm. He was the other interview she had to conduct, so she would just take a peek while she was there. She was stretching her assignment, and she knew it. Knew it and didn't care.

After speaking to all the employees, Cara had turned up nothing out of the ordinary, nothing of real value. She took out the business card Watterson had given her and pulled out her cell phone. She dialed the first three numbers, then disconnected the call and put her phone away. She knew that it was hard to put someone off when she was standing in your office.

It was three o'clock when she arrived at Iverly's office—correction—offices. A ten-story building with the name *Iverly Holdings* in huge letters was a little more than she was expecting. She was directed to the top floor after the security guard verified her identification. This was no retired grandpa there for a smile and a "please sign in." This guy was there for "show me your identification and just maybe I won't boot your ass out the door."

When she stepped off the elevator on the top floor, she was met by a very pert redhead named Valerie. She seemed to be a little more intimidated by her badge than the security guard had been. Valerie informed her that Mr. Iverly was out of town. Cara had been warned, but hoped that he had returned by now. She would have been suspicious that he was just hiding from her if Valerie hadn't also told her he would be back today, and his first stop was always the office. Cara left the building and checked her watch; if the red-haired secretary was right, Iverly should be back by seven.

With nearly four hours to kill, Cara returned to the station and poured over reports. Cops were shaking down every narc, junkie, informant, and hobo that might have ever been in the area. Looking for witnesses, anything.

They had found no fingerprints at the crime scene, except the employees' of course. Autopsy conclusions, noticeably tentative, were that the wound was inflicted with a smooth, extremely sharp weapon. Danny was good and he hadn't even gotten a shot off. She also knew it wasn't a junkie looking for drugs or cash. No hyped-up junkie would be in full control. No, this perpetrator was quiet and stealthy like a shadow that could sweep in.

Cara examined the crime scene photos again with an objective eye. Then she turned to the statements taken by other officers and compared them with her own. No discrepancies. Nothing, nothing, and still nothing. Cara glanced at her watch and decided it was time to go.

On her way out the door it finally struck her where she had seen Thomas' eyes. She'd seen that vacant look on the bodies at the morgue.

CHAPTER 3

Cara arrived at the offices of Mr. Jonathan Iverly at a quarter after seven. She identified herself to the guard who was almost identical to the first, and had to wait for verification before he would release her to ride up the elevator.

She was almost to the top floor when her instincts kicked in again full force. The elevator doors slid open just as Jonathan entered the outer office. Their eyes met for a fraction of a second before they both focused on the man who stood between them. He was like no human Cara had ever encountered. Though neither hideous nor disfigured, something menacing oozed from him. As the man shifted to face her, Cara threw up every shield available to her. She blocked, from both men, her awareness of how terribly wrong everything that surrounded this man seemed to be and her sense that it was somehow familiar to her. His eyes burned into her and seemed not only to memorize her face, but to attempt to pull something from her.

He wasn't big enough to be intimidating, as if Cara was ever intimidated by size alone. He was five foot eleven at best. His skin was a pasty shade of white, but everything else about him was black. Black hair and black eyes set into a long face. He was perhaps thirty-five years old, but those black eyes were ancient and empty. The object in her pocket heated almost unbearably and Cara closed her hand around it.

"Excuse me. I'm Detective Cara Evens. Looking for Jonathan Iverly."

"I'll be with you in a moment, Detective. Just let me deal with this gentleman first." Jonathan's smile was so cold that his face seemed almost brittle.

"I'm sure you remember me," the man growled. "Christian Black. I can see you're busy. I'll call Valerie and make an appointment." Jonathan's face changed at the mention of his secretary's name. Mr. Black turned and left in the elevator with a speed and dexterity that amazed the veteran police officer.

Jonathan ushered her into his office and excused himself under the guise of getting refreshments. Alone, Cara sat in Jonathan's office and took mental inventory of its contents, including the things that were not there. The furniture was impressive and expensive but there were no plaques, diplomas, or pictures of a personal nature. Just pens, pencils, paper, and a computer. She glanced at the door. No, she'd never have enough time to take a peek. It was also unethical. She always went by the book, but then again she wasn't sure how far she was willing to bend the rules to catch Danny's killer. Cara pulled her cell phone out and called the station. When she was connected with Barry she asked him to run Christian Black through the database. Just as she hung up Jonathan came in.

"Now, Detective Evens, what can I do for you?" Uncannily, Jonathan wore the same blank look Thomas did. Cara wondered if that was going to be her lot at every turn with this case; blank stares and empty answers.

"I was quite certain that Mr. Watterson would have informed you of my inquiries." An almost undetectable twitch of his lips told her she was right.

"I was impossible to reach today, but he did leave a message with the office that you would probably want to speak with me."

"I need some information about the employees. Then I would like to see a list of donors and recipients. Mr. Watterson said a copy of those records is kept here." Cara felt like she was under a microscope.

"I can let you see the employee records, but I'm not sure about donors or recipients. I'll have to check with the legal department on that one." He turned toward his computer and began bringing up the employee files.

"Mr. Iverly—" Cara began, but she didn't have a chance to start her battery of questions before he interrupted.

"Jonathan," he said absentmindedly.

Cara looked up from her notes to survey the man in front of her. Rarely was anyone so friendly to the police, especially someone who knew he was going to be questioned closely. Admittedly, he was very attractive. His midnight black hair contrasted with his crystal blue eyes. Everyone always seemed taller than she, and Jonathan was no different at what she estimated to be six foot two. He must find the time to work out. His broad shoulders, trim waist, and strong thighs didn't come from sitting behind a desk.

She surmised that he was obviously just trying to get on her good side. Thomas should have warned him she didn't have one. "Mr. Iverly, do you have any reason to believe that this was not a random act?" Cara had returned to her notes and glanced up when she realized he had stopped typing but hadn't answered her question. He was staring at her as if she had just slapped him in the face.

"I was under the impression that when someone offers the use of their first name, you use it or comment otherwise."

"My apologies. I prefer if we keep this strictly business." Cara saw the shock on his face. He was used to controlling people.

"Actually, I have a few phone calls to make before it gets too late. If you would like to go over the employee files now, I'll be happy to answer your questions later." He reached behind him, took the papers from the printer, and handed them to her. As Cara reached to take the papers from his hand, their fingers touched. Immediately the office fell away and was replaced by an atmosphere totally foreign to Cara. The light was dim: she realized that the only sources were a few thick candles and a lantern. Despair choked her. A fireplace nearby had been left to smolder, and a man sat in front of it with his head in his hands. It was Jonathan.

Jonathan drew his hand away from her and the office came back into focus.

"Thank you," was all she said as she turned to seat herself at the small conference table in the corner. She began making notes. Jonathan probably assumed she was going over the files, but she was writing down everything she could remember from the vision. *I thought it was gone*, kept running through her mind. This was the second time she'd been assaulted by visions in two weeks. She thought the wall she'd built had been strong enough to put it behind her. She was wrong.

CHAPTER 4

Jonathan excused himself for his "phone calls." Shocked, he sat in his secretary's chair and closed his eyes. She couldn't be like him. He would have sensed her the moment she entered the building. If she were human, she could hide her thoughts and emotions better than any he had ever seen and what on God's green earth had made him offer the use of his first name. He never did that; people didn't get close if you didn't let them.

He hadn't thought about it before, but when faced with Christian, she didn't even quiver. Every person he had ever seen in that situation, even those without a drop of intuition, shrank from Christian and the evil that radiated from him. This woman obviously had more than an average dose of intuition.

She had seen. He knew she had. With a simple touch, she had pulled a memory from him that he hadn't let himself think about in years.

The others had told him so many lies about what he was. They knew he couldn't be fully trusted, that he had only been turned physically. He received most of his education through watching them. Try as he might, he couldn't seem to hone his abilities as the others had. There was something they weren't telling him. There was a reason they didn't kill him, though he couldn't discern what it was. Cruelty seemed to be acceptable. When the group was lacking in entertainment they would subdue him and drain him to the point of death. Vampires heal quickly and this task was time consuming as well as excruciating for

Jonathan. When he was out of his mind with hunger they would set him free. Jonathan became adept at escaping, hiding and fighting. In the end the pain that Jonathan inflicted on those seeking entertainment outweighed the enjoyment they received in watching him slowly starve. He endured hours of torture, always waiting to repay the favor.

Ten years after he'd been changed from a husband and father to a widower and a vampire, he was still planning and watching. One of their "helpers" came just before dawn to warn him that the villagers were gathering to hunt them down. Jonathan had known the others had fed too long on this village, but they refused to let themselves fear humans—they were, after all, nothing more than a source for food. Jonathan sent the man away but didn't give the others his warning.

Since Jonathan spent as much time as possible away from the brood, he had already established a sanctuary in case of such an uprising. He would not stand by the pack or fight with them. On the other hand, the villagers would never accept his help; they would kill him before they would hear him out.

On his way to the cave entrance he passed Christian's alcove. Though he could have been heading to join the others, Christian must have sensed something because he stopped Jonathan and pulled him inside. Christian threw him to the ground and demanded to know what he was planning. A fight ensued. Christian underestimated Jonathan's strength, and in a short time Jonathan turned the tables and threw Christian to the ground. Jonathan stood waiting for Christian to get up. It took him a minute to realize that Christian had landed on a spike that protruded from the floor. It had pierced his heart. Jonathan turned to run from the room, knowing that sound traveled easily in the caves and the others would be on him in seconds.

A humming caught his attention. Something on the inside wall of Christian's alcove. He ran his hand over the wall. What had once faded into the gray of the stone turned a blood red. It was a book that Jonathan took and left.

He reached his sanctuary with barely enough time to escape both the sunlight and the angry villagers. He heard them coming and heard the screams of the pack being overrun by a thousand humans. He caught himself praying that they would not come for him, and then thought, *does it matter?* Jonathan thought of all he'd endured waiting for the right time to take his revenge. All that he'd done to survive. He remembered his wife, his daughter and the goodness that had been in both. Should he walk into the sun and have it be over? He tried in those few hours to work out the reason for his existence and he came to the conclusion that most reach when trying to solve such dilemmas. He had no specific idea why he was there or exactly what he was to do with the life he was given, but Jonathan knew that giving up was wrong. Throwing away his life was not the answer. A few hours wasn't nearly enough time to answer the question of existence but Jonathan had all the time in the world to solve life's biggest question and perhaps do justice to the gifts he'd been given.

When the screaming ended, he ventured out to see the carnage that was left behind. Jonathan knew it had only taken the sunlight moments to reduce the bodies to skeletons. Apparently the villagers weren't sure how to kill vampires because some were still in the caves, decapitated and mutilated. He counted twenty or so bodies and knew that some had escaped. The faces on most were badly damaged.

Jonathan went deep into the cave in search of Christians' body, but it was gone, replaced by a message left in Christians' alcove. I'LL COME FOR YOU.

CHAPTER 5

Cara finished making her notes from the employee files and stepped into the outer office. She had found nothing that seemed immediately obvious, but sometimes connections only revealed themselves after a bit of hard study. Jonathan still sat at his secretary's desk, breathing comfortably, but was otherwise quite motionless. She checked her watch: it was after ten. He was probably exhausted after his business trip. She almost felt sorry for him.

Cara stepped softly beside him and gently grasped his shoulder to wake him. The second she touched him her mind exploded with fierce intensity: a clearing at the foot of a mountain; caves leading into darkness; charred bones littering a once peaceful forest. The remains gave her a very clear picture of how much pain was involved in these deaths; skeletal faces frozen forever in fear. Hands clasped together, praying for mercy. Cara heard a rising whine and turned, but no living creature was to be seen. The whine grew louder and changed into a thousand voices screaming in agony. An odor attacked her nostrils, the acrid smell of burning flesh. The screaming escalated inside her head to the point that she didn't notice Jonathan gasp and jerk away from her touch. She could not have felt his movement, the pain was so vivid and disturbing.

As quickly as it had appeared, the vision vanished from her mind, but the voices echoed still. Dazed, she saw Jonathan rise and move towards her. Instinctively she backed away, dropping both her briefcase and her purse but not her guard. Her hands came up to cover her ears, but when a final piercing cry stabbed through her she closed her eyes and slid to the ground.

Jonathan effortlessly picked up her limp body and reflected for only a moment on the way she had retreated from him in fear. He knew what she had seen was a tremendous shock even though she was a cop and used to dealing with the gruesome. If he was correct, she was also incredibly empathic; able to fully experience the emotions of others.

He took Cara to his car and buckled her in. When he arrived at his apartment building carrying her through the door, he grinned at the doorman and received a wink as he was buzzed through. He laid her on the couch and had the uncomfortable and unusual feeling of not knowing what to do. He knew he could easily enter her sleeping mind, but at this point he didn't know how many invasions she could take. She seemed unusually strong, but Jonathan didn't want to make unnecessary assumptions. After an hour he decided he had no choice but to go in after her.

Kneeling beside her, he took her hand and began by placing himself in the image she'd pulled from him. She was no longer there. Cautiously he made his way to his own sanctuary. She had found it. She was gazing at three glowing balls rotating in the air.

"Cara?" He spoke quietly, reassuringly.

"Go away." She looked up at him and the balls disappeared.

"You don't belong here. You have to leave this place." He didn't move any closer to her.

"It's so loud out there . . . and it hurts. I don't want to leave." Her voice was childlike. "I can't leave until it's strong enough."

"I'll help you. You don't have to go alone." He didn't know what she was talking about, but he thought it odd that she accepted his presence.

"Can you make it go away? Can you make him stop?" Desperation poured out through her voice, and he got the feeling that they were no longer talking about the massacre she had seen.

"It has stopped, Cara. It's not real. It happened a very long time ago." He slowly held out his hand and waited. She gazed at it for a long time, and finally got to her feet and took it.

He walked with her until they stood in front of the battle site, and then turned her away from it to face him.

"You have to come the rest of the way by yourself. I'll be waiting for you. Come back to me now, Cara." She cocked her head to the side as if questioning his choice of words. He couldn't blame her. He could have chosen a hundred different things to say, but the truth was that he did want her back with him. "Close your eyes and concentrate on me."

Cara could feel him slip from her mind and was suddenly drowning and clawing her way to the surface; swimming through layers of pain and anger. She was half-asleep yet acutely awake. Just when she thought she could last no longer and would rather sink into the oblivion, she came to full consciousness, keeping her eyes closed. After another minute, she took a deep breath to assure herself she was grounded in reality once more. She thought it was strange how the feeling of being held by Jonathan lingered until she opened her eyes and saw that she was sitting in his lap. His head was tipped back against the sofa, eyes closed as if he were sleeping innocently. Of course, he had looked that way once before, and she saw where that had gotten her.

Cara stirred to remove herself from Jonathan's lap. His head came up and she froze.

"Cara?" Jonathan's voice still sounded as if he were consoling a wounded child.

"Who did you expect?" Cara attempted a smile, it was a little crooked but it worked. Cara felt all her armor sliding back into place and removed herself from Jonathan's lap and stood.

"You must be feeling better." Jonathan returned her smile with one just as unsure.

Cara wanted answers. She was always looking for answers. Her most important question at the moment was *why is this resurfacing?*

Jonathan looked over her tousled curls and rumpled clothes.

"Why are you looking at me like that?" Cara's eyes narrowed.

Jonathan blinked. "Just thinking. It's almost two in the morning. We should probably get you home. I'm sure you need some rest."

She was still eyeing him warily but nodded. "I have a car. I can drive myself."

For the first time she took in her surroundings. His apartment was adorned, just as his office was, with the bare necessities, nothing personal.

"This is my apartment, Cara. Your car is back at the offices."

"Why did you bring me here?"

"I didn't know how long it was going to take you to come out of wherever you went to. I figured Valerie might have gotten upset if she came to work and found an unconscious woman lying on the floor."

"Please call me a taxi and I'll go pick up my car."

Jonathan started to argue but must have realized it would be futile. He buzzed the doorman to call her a taxi and waited with her in the lobby until it came. Silently they waited, and when she saw the yellow cab pull up at the curb she left without saying a word.

CHAPTER 6

Cara made it home safely after she picked up her car from the empty lot at Iverly Holdings. Her apartment seemed small compared to Jonathan's, but it also looked like someone lived there. The hamper seemed entirely too far away, so she dropped her clothes beside the bed and crawled in. She lay there and wondered why her system wasn't in shock. She supposed it was because her life had never been normal. Life was always throwing her curve balls.

Even though she had been unconscious much of the last four hours, the experience had left her exhausted. As she drifted off she thought about that first incident in Jonathan's office, and something she had noticed right off came back to her; the clothes, the entire set up, it all seemed so antiquated. What did it mean? Was he roughing it? Did he have a cabin somewhere in the middle of nowhere? Then what about his clothes? The second glimpse into Jonathan's mind was even more alarming. A war perhaps? Her weary mind could take no more; her final conscious thought was that hopefully Jonathan wouldn't mention his bizarre encounter with her to the detectives assigned to Danny's case.

In the basement of Cara's building, Christian hid from the sunlight. Smiling, he tuned himself in to her. He could hear her heartbeat and feel her life force. He had searched a long time for Jonathan, and the time for retribution had come. Christian still feared the consequences of killing Jonathan, but he had an idea, a loop hole, and Cara had just made herself a part of his plan. Jonathan had tried to block it, but Christian had caught his first reaction to Cara. "Chemistry", humans called it. Judging from the amount of time she had spent in Jonathan's apartment, it must have been quite strong. Cara was a power too. Whether she knew it or not, she possessed some gift. He could use it. Although he was about to come into a great deal of power he could always use more.

The wait for revenge was eating at Christian, but being able to torture those around Jonathan made it easier. He would wait, indeed must wait, until Cara became a bit more important to Jonathan.

CHAPTER 7

Cara awoke rejuvenated when her alarm clock went off. It was ten o'clock, and though she hadn't gotten home until four she felt full of energy. She had focus now, a purpose. After a week of sitting and wondering, Cara finally had an avenue to investigate. She showered and dressed in a pair of black slacks and a sleeveless sweater. Cara rarely dressed for fashion; comfort and being able to move freely were foremost in her mind. The fact that her clothes tended to conform to her figure, making her more alluring, was a very distant side benefit that only occasionally crossed her mind.

Cara went to her car in the parking garage. As she unlocked the driver's side door, she sensed that someone was watching her, but when she discreetly, and then openly, looked around she could see no one. Most of the people who lived in the building were already gone for the day, so there were very few cars to block her view. When she was satisfied that there was nobody in sight, she got into the car and drove to work. She had two priorities that day. One, try to find out what progress had been made on Danny's investigation. Two, go see Beth.

Beth Giddens was Cara's closest friend. They had been friends from childhood. Blessed with an incredibly quick and insightful mind, Beth was often helpful with Cara's work. Now she was hoping that Beth could help her with the visions; specifically she hoped she could help her to figure out why Jonathan had been dressed in knee britches. She'd put the visit off long enough. She hesitated because the main reason Cara needed to see Beth was the object in her pocket. Beth would certainly be able to identify it. Cara didn't want to lead danger to Beth's door, but could feel the urgency of the thing, it's barely restrained need to be used. Just the fact that she was receiving emotions from a *thing* was enough to make her uneasy.

Cara entered the station just in time to see Mason slam the captain's door. He glanced at Cara and made a bee-line for her. She looked over her shoulder to see who Mason was going to kill. By the expression on his face, that was surely his intent. Unfortunately, she didn't see anyone standing behind her.

"What the hell do you think you're doing?" Mason had his jaw clamped so tightly it might have been wired shut.

"I just got here." Cara decided to play it cool until she knew what was going on. However, she was pleased that Mason's feelings weren't piercing her armor. She had been afraid that she had lost some of her control after last night, but apparently not.

"You're fucking with things you have no business being anywhere near. I know the captain slid you some of the reports and gave you interviews, but I'm sure we can find you a meter maid shift if you feel like you don't have enough to do." Mason had started out in a low growl, but his voice had risen and other officers were beginning to stare.

"I don't know what you're talking about. The only thing I'm investigating is Danny's murder." Cara kept her voice low.

"Really, well why don't you explain why you ran Christian Black through Barry last night." Mason had noticed the attention they were attracting and lowered his voice back to a rumble.

"When I went to Iverly's office last night he was there. There was something going on between them, and I wanted to get information about the both of them." Cara's jaw began to ache, and she realized she was clamping her teeth together.

In an instant Mason's anger wiped from his face. Replacing it was sheer disbelief. He opened and shut his mouth twice before looking around for an empty interrogation room and quickly pulled her in.

Cara tensed as she saw Mason's hand coming toward her. She relaxed when she only sensed a few of his emotions; primarily excitement and anticipation.

"Run that by me again. You met him? What did he look like? Was he Italian? Columbian?"

"Mason! You just chewed my ass out in front of the entire station. What is going on?"

Mason stared at her a moment as if considering something. "Dizzazio has been getting suspicious, especially since the snafu with Vinton. He knows something is going on but Dizzazio thinks the competition is going to make a move on him, so he's brought in Christian Black. This guy is a heavy hitter; you want someone dead, they're dead, and it's never pretty. We don't have much on him, mostly just through the grapevine. It's like that guy in that movie, I don't remember the name, but just a whisper here and there. You look for him and poof, he's gone. You, my dear, are the first person I've heard of that's ever seen him."

Cara crossed her arms over her chest, waiting for the other shoe to drop. She ran over everything in her mind. *Shit.* There weren't very many reasons for a man like Christian Black to be at a powerful businessman's office at night when no one was around. Like a simple operation that somehow went awry when a policeman showed up. She didn't know exactly how it went down, but she was sure now it had involved both Jonathan and Christian.

"You know it probably has nothing to do with Danny." Mason stopped looking her in the eye. He had shoved his hands in his pockets like a small boy about to get in big trouble.

"That would be a great big coincidence." She had a feeling she knew what was coming.

"Captain Monahan is putting you on a desk until we have more information. If you go after Black both he and Dizzazio will get spooked. We've worked on this for the last eighteen months and we can't have any mistakes." Mason sounded like he didn't relish being the one to deliver the news.

"That's bullshit!" Cara exploded.

"A lot of money and man power has gone into this case. If we get Black this way, you can always find out if he had anything to do with Danny's murder later." He was trying to sound reasonable, but he had to know he wasn't getting through.

"He was a cop, damn it. I don't think so." Cara spun around and jerked the door open. Mason put out a hand to stop her, and the look she threw him was enough to halt him. The violence in her whispered, "Don't touch me!" and he backed up a step.

"I need you to get with a sketch artist." Cara closed the door slowly and turned to face him. "I can make you stay." Mason's voice hardened. Criminals were usually the only ones treated to the unbending quality that could be heard in Mason's words. "You're a witness in my investigation. I can hold you with that."

She wanted to hurt him. Cara pulled her anger in and held it. Fingers uncurled from fists, shoulders relaxing down, expression clearing. "Why?" Cara cocked her head to the side.

"Why what?"

"Why would you want me to sit with a sketch artist?" Her confusion was so genuine Mason blinked.

"So you can give a composite of Christian Black."

"Who?"

"Don't play me Cara. Barry can back me up. He took the call from you asking for a run on Black."

"He must have misunderstood me. I've never heard of this person."

"Don't do this Cara." Mason's face dropped when Cara flashed him a cat-like smile.

Cara walked out of the room and heads turned. She ignored them and kept walking until she reached her car. Sliding into the front seat, she fired up the engine and headed home. When she arrived there she sat in her car for a moment and took several deep breaths. The anger was still there; she cultivated it and stored it until it was no longer at the surface.

Heading up to her apartment, she changed clothes, pulling on a pair of black leggings and another sleeveless sweater—this one black with a turtleneck. She switched her pumps for a pair of black boots and tucked her gun in the small of her back before pulling her top over it. Her clothes often reflected her mood, and this one was definitely dark.

Breathing a bit more evenly now, Cara went into the living room and sat on the sofa. She would have to wait. She couldn't put her plan into motion just yet. She focused by closing her eyes. She wasn't only slipping into something more comfortable and relaxing, she was preparing for battle.

CHAPTER 8

Modern superstition leads people to believe that vampires sleep in coffins, but Jonathan had found he could sleep just about anywhere. He preferred his bed. The truth was that sleep wasn't something he needed a lot of, although he went to bed every morning—it made him feel somewhat human to have an ordinary habit.

Unbidden, his thoughts centered on Cara as he lay there. He was definitely attracted to her, but was that all? Could he afford to be interested? How had she come into this gift of hers? Question after question went through his mind until he decided he had enough on his plate without throwing in hormones.

Focusing on Christian, he began to toss, driving all hopes of sleep from his restless body. Jonathan was no longer the hotheaded young man bent on revenge. These days he plotted meticulously. He was accused of being ruthless and immovable in the boardroom. If Christian continued in this vein, harming those few that were close to Jonathan, he would find out that business was child's play compared to Jonathan's other strengths.

After hours of tossing, sleep overcame him. Jonathan's dreams were painful in their clarity. Each memory of those early days was still so vivid that the horror of it all eventually woke him, and he had to force himself to remember that it had happened a long time ago. The image of his wife and daughter brutally slain had been a recurring nightmare for decades, but he hadn't had it in years.

Jonathan opened his eyes and looked at his sparse surroundings. His windowless bedroom had only a large bed. It needed to be easy for him to move on, should it be necessary. As he lay there, he could feel the strength of the sun bearing down on the walls of his penthouse.

Cara entered his thoughts once again. He thought of how different she was, even beyond her abilities. There was something inside her that almost glowed with intensity. She was unaware of it, but it was visible to him, and if he could see it so could Christian.

He could easily imagine her waging war by his side against the enemy that had taken something from both of them. He wondered what it would be like to have someone to spend an eternity with and then he stopped his thoughts. *No one deserves this. To be cursed forever. Trapped and free at the same time. Free to explore and experience, but trapped into being a monster.*

He shook himself from his maudlin thoughts and got up. The sun was going down and he could sense the earth cooling. He settled himself at his desk burying his thoughts in work. Two centuries ago you could conduct business with a handshake. Today a mountain of paperwork and an army of attorneys seemed to accompany every deal. A few hours into legal jargon he realized that in his haste his briefcase had been left at the office the night before. This deal was to close soon and the last contract he had to review was still in his briefcase. He gathered the contracts he would need, set them by his keys and headed to the shower. He wasn't sure what Christian's next move would be, but he had watchers out trying to cover anyone that Christian might target.

The last person he expected to see when he opened his door was Cara. She wasn't only glowing, she was practically vibrating.

"How did you get up here?"

For the second night in a row he seemed unsure how to react to her.

"Your doorman recognized me." Her voice was calm, but something was definitely up.

He stood aside so she could enter. He had a feeling it wasn't a good idea but couldn't see any other option.

She crossed the threshold and stood in the middle of the room.

"I suppose I'll need to have a talk with him. He really should call before he sends someone up." He was making small talk and failing miserably. Crossing to a sideboard he turned his back to her under the pretense of making himself a drink. "Can I get you anything?" He turned and saw that she had adopted a fighter's stance. Feet slightly spread, firmly planted, and arms hanging loosely, seemingly carelessly, at her sides.

"Don't you usually have someone do your dirty work, I'm sorry; your talking, for you?" The air around her crackled with tension.

"Excuse me?"

"Isn't that what Christian is for? He does all the nasty deeds you don't want to be involved with. I know who and what he is, and you two are of the same breed. Just because your hands don't get bloody doesn't make you any less of a monster." Her voice was rough, and he knew they were both going to lose it in a moment. His hand constricted around the glass until it shattered.

"What did you say?" he whispered. To hear the words come from her tore through him.

"I didn't stutter. I said you were a monster." She had seen the effect her words had on him and zeroed in. Jonathan moved lightning quick and was standing a breath away from her in a split second. Despite her surprise she didn't back down. Her chin simply went up another notch.

"Do you think this has been easy for me? Do you think this is a life I chose?" His anger rose to meet hers.

"Everyone has a choice and must answer for their decisions."

"Really? Let me show you what my choices were!" he ground out. Jonathan grabbed her by the shoulders and unleashed on her something he never wished on anyone. He brought up the memory of finding the mutilated bodies of his family and forced it into her mind. He transferred all the pain and despair into her to make her pay for her condemnation. He gave her the turning of his soul, the slaughter of his own humanity and all the anguish that accompanied it.

Her scream penetrated the haze of rage flowing through him, and he opened his eyes. He expected to feel vindicated, but when he saw her unfocused gaze and the tears streaming down her face he only felt like . . .well...a monster.

He still held her shoulders and suddenly her thoughts broke through his. Some were jumbled images of what had led her here, but one thought was clear: *I didn't know. I didn't know.* She hadn't even been close to the truth until he had shown her.

Cara's mind reeled from the images. The pain emanating from Jonathan turned her inside out. Her body was either on fire or numb, she couldn't quite tell. She felt herself being maneuvered to a leather chair. He left her for a scant moment and returned with a glass. He held it to her lips, and she instinctively drank in the warm liquid. She blinked several times and her vision cleared. She must have been numb, because the feeling began to return to her limbs. Jonathan kneeled before her, and though her mouth opened, nothing came out. She was still trying to organize what she should say. Jonathan reached out and stroked her cheek; she flinched away. He rose in a swift movement, his jaw clenched.

"You still think I'm a monster? Then what makes you think I'll let you leave?" His voice was hoarse with three centuries of pain.

Jonathan stiffened as Cara reached out for his hand; she turned it over and showed him the small pieces of glass that had been embedded in it.

"No, Jonathan, I don't think you're a monster."

He looked from his hand to her cheek. "Where do we go from here?"

Cara felt as if her emotions had been stripped and wondered how much she could take before total collapse.

Jonathan looked again at his hand, then sat down on the edge of the couch and turned his eyes to her. He was searching for something, looking confused. Silently, he knelt before her once more. His gaze fastened on her lips, and he moved closer. She didn't move away.

His lips were warm, the pressure was light, and Cara felt herself instinctively lean into him. His mouth opened ever so gently and she followed suit. The touch of his tongue on hers sent tremors through her. She slid her arms around his neck and pulled herself into his embrace. His hands slid from her shoulders to her waist and pulled her toward him until their bodies met. They couldn't get any closer as Jonathan's hips were cradled between Cara's thighs. Her blood warmed as Jonathan kneaded her backside; she wanted to get closer. *This man can kiss!*

"Thank you." Jonathan rasped and she was gone in a flash. She now had her body pressed against the back of the chair instead of against him, and her legs were no longer wrapped around him but curled against her chest.

"I didn't say that out loud." Cara didn't mind getting other people's thoughts, but the idea that someone could read hers did not sit well with her.

"I didn't do it intentionally, Cara. You can trust me. You know more about me than almost anyone now. I need you to tell me what you are. Are you human?"

"Of course, I'm human. What kind of a question is that?" Cara asked incredulously.

"I've never met a human who had powers of the mind like you. I haven't been human for about three centuries now, so please don't make it sound like the end of the world." He was insulted. He gripped the arms of the chair and brought himself closer to her.

"I didn't mean it like that. You made it sound as if antennas were going to sprout out of my head." Cara unwound herself and put her palm on his face. "You're more human than you think. I can feel it."

Jonathan looked sorely tempted to kiss her again. Instead, he pulled her hand away from his face and returned it to her lap. "I think you should go home, pack, and find someplace quiet until this all goes away."

"Find someplace quiet?" She came up from her seat, forcing him to his feet. "This mind thing works both ways, remember. I'm not going to sit somewhere and twiddle my thumbs while he runs around loose."

He held up a hand. "You don't know what you're dealing with or how many."

"I'll find a way," she said with no doubt in her mind.

"Cara, you can't fight him." He took a step toward her, and she backed away. That stopped him.

Cara turned to go and he let her. He would have someone watching her anyway. The door shut behind her, and Jonathan stood in the middle of the room for a moment, then cleaned the broken glass from the floor. After throwing it in the trash, he picked up the phone. He turned his head toward the door, something felt wrong. He ignored it and dialed Thomas' number. He was probably feeling apprehensive about letting Cara leave alone, but the feeling was growing stronger.

Thomas picked up the phone and started speaking just as all of Jonathan's senses hit red alert. He uttered a terse, "Call you back" and hung up the phone. He threw open his door, got in the elevator, and headed toward the underground garage.

As soon as the elevator doors slid open, Jonathan knew Christian had been there. He spotted an empty parking slot and knew that was where Cara's car had been. He ran toward the spot and saw two sets of footprints in the dirt and grime that covered the concrete. Cara's smaller prints backed up against the car and a larger pair looked to be standing close to her, much too close.

This time he took the stairs and literally flew into his apartment and snatched up the phone. He hit redial and Thomas picked up before the first ring was finished. "What the hell is going on?"

"Cara just left my building. She encountered Christian in the garage." Jonathan explained, trying to keep his voice level.

"What was she doing there?" Thomas wasn't used to being kept out of the loop. For the last eighty years Thomas had known everything Jonathan did.

"Find out where she lives. I want to make sure she's okay." He knew Thomas wasn't a fan of Cara, but he had to know she was all right. "She knows. That makes her a threat to Christian. I'll explain everything later. Just find out where she is."

There was a pause on the line. "I'll find out where she lives, but you realize Christian isn't the only one she's a threat to." Jonathan knew that Thomas feared the inevitable, that sooner or later someone would find out about them. If all Jonathan was worried about was Cara's safety then he must have reason to believe she wouldn't blow them out of the water. He felt some of his anger slide away; he feared for Jonathan though. Jonathan was powerful but he could still be killed. Death for Thomas would be inconvenient, but he could come back.

They disconnected and Jonathan knew there was only one reason Cara would have walked away alive. Christian wanted to change her.

CHAPTER 9

I t was almost six hours before Jonathan's phone rang.

"Iverly." Thomas' voice was clipped. To Jonathan it seemed as if a century had passed since they had spoken, and he knew what a century felt like. It had been midmorning when Cara left and now the afternoon had settled in. He couldn't go to her now. If what he believed was true, the hours that separated them wouldn't matter anyway.

"I found her. I'm outside her apartment now. Do you have any idea how hard it is to find a police officer's address?" Jonathan could hear the unease in Thomas' voice. Something wasn't right.

"Is she there?" Jonathan gripped the receiver so hard it might have split in half.

"Her car was here so I went to her door. I can hear something inside but she won't respond. Maybe because it's me, but I don't think so. All the shades are drawn." He said the latter quietly. "Do you want me to go in?"

"No. It doesn't matter now. I'll leave at six and I'll meet you there." He said good-bye and threw the phone in the direction of where it should have been hung up. He stared at it for a moment, then picked it up carefully and set it in its cradle. It was still two hours before he could leave—the sun would not be down completely, but the tinting of the car windows was enough to protect him. He looked toward the one window in his penthouse, saw the fringes of sunlight beaming around the black shades, and cursed his prison.

Jonathan checked his inner clock as well as the one on his wrist and decided to leave a few minutes early, driven by a pounding need to get there. As he drove, the possibility that Christian had changed Cara into a slave crossed his mind—no will of her own and at Christian's beck and call. He dismissed the idea. She had too much power within her; to make her into a slave he would have to kill her first. His pondering was put aside as he parked beside her car in the parking garage of her building. Thomas was there waiting for him.

"Let's go." Jonathan broke into a run with Thomas close behind. As they reached the stairwell Jonathan became a blur.

He reached Cara's door and stopped to listen. He could hear movement inside, and a low moan reached his sensitive ears. Leaning his head against the door, he feared the worst. He lifted his head and scanned the hallway to make sure he was alone. Thomas came around the corner panting.

"I wish you wouldn't do that. You make me look bad." He was trying to lighten the mood. It hadn't worked.

Jonathan twisted the doorknob and broke the lock. The dead bolt gave with a little nudge. Thomas put the doorknob back together so it didn't look suspicious while Jonathan headed toward the bedroom. It was a one-bedroom apartment, it wasn't hard to find. He opened the door, then took a half step back and closed his eyes in a vain attempt to shut out the pain that suddenly whipped through his body. He heard Thomas come up behind him and inhale sharply.

He had hoped that this wasn't what he would find. Cara was in the middle of the bed wearing only a T-shirt and panties. Her blankets were tangled around her writhing body. Her hands clutched the sheet. Soul-shattering sobs came from deep in her throat as her back arched off the bed. Her face contorted in pain. Teeth marks scarred her neck. She was changing.

"What now?" Thomas asked softly.

"We wait. If she retains enough of her humanity, then we help her; if not . . ." he let the sentence fall away. He didn't know if he had it within himself to tear her heart out. Maybe this was Christian's master plan. If Jonathan killed her, and he would have to, he would no longer be in Christian's way. "I'll see how far she has to go."

Jonathan sat on the edge of Cara's bed and pulled one of her grasping hands loose from its grip on the sheet. She grabbed hold with a fierce grip. He knew he would feel her pain; he believed he deserved it. Images and emotions slammed into him. He kept his hold on her as long as he could, but her emotions were reaching their peak. Suddenly he was literally blown away as the force of her agony threw him from the bed and against the nearby wall.

Jonathan slid to the floor, and Thomas started toward the bed.

"No!" Jonathan yelled, knowing his friend's intent. "Don't touch her!" He pulled himself to his feet and went to Thomas. "She's not changing." As they watched from the foot of the bed, Cara stopped writhing and slowly sat up.

Cara looked at Jonathan and Thomas standing in her bedroom, and was probably wondering why they were there. She brought her hands up to her head as though trying to keep it from falling off her shoulders. Jonathan went into her adjoining bathroom and retrieved some aspirin and a glass of water. After he fed it to her, she collapsed back onto her bed. She gazed at him for a moment and then her eyes slid closed.

They watched her until it seemed she was sleeping peacefully. Jonathan motioned with his head for Thomas to follow him out. They shut the door as they left the bedroom and went to the small kitchen and dining room off of her living room. Thomas was waiting impatiently, but in silence, until Jonathan saw he could stand it no longer. "What was that?" He was intent. Like he'd never seen anything like that before.

"A nightmare, Thomas. What you saw was nothing but a nightmare." Jonathan looked at Thomas. He had reservations about telling Cara's secrets.

"*That was a nightmare?*" Thomas was thunderstruck.

Jonathan said, "It was a nightmare, of sorts. Cara is psychic. Well, she's more than that, she's also empathic. When I touched her she was having a dream. I think she was born with these abilities, but when she was young she only picked up strong emotions from people. In her dream she was traveling with her father to a house; I think it was in her neighborhood because I didn't get that he was there officially. He was a police officer." Thomas was eyeing him strangely, and Jonathan knew he was making a mess of it.

"I'm sorry, but I got all this in a very short burst, and it's hard to make sense of it all. Okay, the home belonged to the parents of a missing girl. While Cara's father talked with them in the kitchen Cara was waiting in the living room. She saw the little girl's teddy bear, picked the bear up and . . ." Jonathan had to stop to take a deep breath. "And she saw the little girl being held in another house not far away. She was being beaten. Badly. Cara screamed for her father and told them where she was. They didn't get there in time."

Thomas leaned forward and put his head in his hands. "And she could see and feel all that?" he asked.

"Yes." Jonathan was somber.

"How old was she? What happened to her after that?"

"Maybe nine or ten. My guess is that afterwards she retreated into her own world and built a wall, something to keep all those emotions from other people out."

"What about what happened just now? How did she slam you into the wall?"

"I think her gifts have morphed. They're changing."

"You're wrong," Cara said from the doorway. "I built that wall so that *I* didn't have to feel anything. No one would ever do to me what they did to her."

"But that's not what happened, Cara." Jonathan stood and Thomas followed. They all moved into the living room. Jonathan knew it had been a long time since Cara had given her emotions free reign, and she looked like she wanted to let them loose now. She looked beyond angry.

"I need to go check with the others. I'll get with you later, Jonathan." Thomas headed for the door.

"And what makes you think I'll let you leave? After all, I have all these changing powers to explore and Jonathan has a few more secrets of mine he can share."

The air around her began to crackle, and just like last night she seemed to vibrate. Jonathan took note and cautiously placed himself between Cara and Thomas. She couldn't kill him but she could hurt him. She didn't look like she had that much control yet over her newfound ability.

"Protecting your friend? How noble!" Cara appeared to be calmer, more in control.

Calmly and evenly Jonathan spoke, "Thomas, go. I'll contact you later." Thomas hesitated and then left, closing the door carefully. Turning to face Cara again, Jonathan continued, "You shouldn't be so hard on him. He came here to help you."

"Help me what? Get in touch with my inner self? Thanks, but no thanks. I was as in touch as I wanted to be."

"We came here because we thought Christian had gotten to you." Jonathan saw a flicker of something in Cara's eyes.

"Well, he didn't. You can go now."

"I want to know what happened. It's important. I need to know what he's planning." He was positive she was hiding something.

"None of your business." She was refusing to be bullied.

"You don't know what you're dealing with. The fact that he got this close to you should prove that to you." His voice rose, but she still wasn't talking. Jonathan's patience snapped.

He flew across the room and scooped her up. They landed on the couch, with him on top, crushing her into the cushions. Jonathan felt her try to block him. Despite her best efforts, the memory he wanted surfaced.

Cara knew Christian was there as soon as the elevator had started to descend. The doors slid open, and there he was, evil incarnate, leaning on the car opposite hers. She took her time and stopped a few feet from her car. Adopting an equally negligent pose, she simply stared at him.

"Well, well, getting a little close to our suspect, aren't you, Detective? That's two nights in a row." Christian's eyes gleamed like a cat ready to pounce.

Cara continued to stare at him with no emotion on her face.

"You know, Miss Evens," he continued, changing how he addressed her. "There's something about you, something I can't quite see. I can usually see an awful lot. I don't get fear from you, I get . . . nothing." As he spoke he drew nearer, his voice like sandpaper. He slid his hand forward and checked the pulse in her neck with his fingers. She felt her heart beating slow and steady against his skin. She didn't flinch. That really pissed him off. He took a strand of hair and spun it between his fingers.

"What, I wonder, would it take to get a reaction out of you?" Christian was distracted for a second by the smile that spread over Cara's lips. That second was all it took for Cara to knee him powerfully in the groin. Even full-fledged vampires couldn't handle a blow like that. He fell to his knees, and Cara liked to think he could see stars as well. She sidestepped him and moved quickly to her car door.

"Nice to see some things affect all men the same," she said over her shoulder. Before she made it to her car, Christian jumped up, seized her, spun her around, and slammed her body into the door.

"Recovery time is much better, however. Do you have any idea what I could do to you? I know you know what I am; I don't know how, but you do. You would be stupid not to fear me." He grabbed her hair, wrenched her head to the side, and sank his teeth into her neck. Her blood was sweet, but something was missing. He lifted his head. Blood dripped from his fangs.

"Fear. Is that what you really want from me? Rip out my throat, tear out my heart, what would that take? Seconds? Would I even feel it? I won't waste my time anticipating death, being afraid. Sorry to be such a disappointment to you, but you'll get nothing from me." Cara vaguely thought she must be insane, but instinct made her lash out.

Christian stared at her lips and she could feel his chest rubbing up against her breasts with each breath. The bastard was getting hard. He lifted her by her arms until they were eye level; her feet didn't touch the ground. Grinding his arousal against her, he put his lips to her ear.

"Do you feel that? There are worse things than death. I could take you in ways you can't even imagine. Anticipate that." He dropped her and stepped away, looking her up and down.

"Any more threats before I go?" Cara struck a casual pose, leaning on her car.

Christian took a step toward her and stopped. No. He turned and disappeared.

Cara got in her car and drove away. For the first time she thanked God for her abilities. Tonight it did seem a gift. She knew in her bones that if Christian had seen one flicker of fear, they wouldn't have been able to find all the pieces of her.

Jonathan released her. He took in the bite marks on her neck and the bruises on her arms. His hands turned to fists as he thought of the way Christian had touched her.

Cara lay silently underneath him. Finally she asked, "Did you get everything you needed?" She began to squirm trying to dislodge him.

"I'm trying to protect you. Cara, stop. Stop moving." Jonathan knew there was no way to hide his body's reaction to her. She noticed and stopped moving.

"Get off me." Cara's voice was level but very lethal. He got up.

He put out a hand to help her up, but her robe had fallen open, showing she was still only in her T-shirt and panties. She slapped his hand away and retied her robe. She crossed the room and reached for the door, but when she pulled, the knob fell off in her hand. Jonathan would have laughed at her expression if she hadn't turned a deadly glare his way.

"Get out." She managed to get the door open and stood beside it.

"Cara, I needed to know. If you're going to go after him you need to learn." He stopped talking when she held up her hand, crossed the room to her and walked out the door.

She spoke before he could. "Let me tell you what I have learned. Vampires, no matter what kind, don't like it when they don't get what they want. If you don't give it to them, they hold you down until you submit. No matter what your motives, your bruises will show the same way Christian's do." He practically snarled at her. "Careful, your fangs are showing," she said sweetly as she slammed the door in his face.

CHAPTER 10

Cara had phoned Captain Monahan when she returned from Jonathan's that morning. Monahan certainly knew she was lying when she told him she was taking all of her leave time because she needed a break. Mason was making it clear he was angry she wouldn't cooperate with his investigation. Jonathan acted irate that she wouldn't put her life in his hands and sit in the background. Thomas, well, he just didn't seem to like her.

She toweled off, and then threw on a pair of jeans and a tank top. There was only one more person that mattered to her—Beth. She would be on her way there soon.

She was just tying her boots when Mason walked into her apartment. "What happened to your door?" He looked at the doorknob that had fallen to the floor when he pushed the door open. It hadn't even been shut all the way.

"Don't ask."

"What happened to your arms and, Jesus, what happened to your neck?"

"A rabid dog. Are we playing the 'what happened' game? I was on my way out."

"Are you going to leave your door like that?" He held his hands up in surrender when she glared at him. "Okay, sorry."

"There's nothing here that's not replaceable."

She looked around suddenly aware that he was checking out her place. On the far wall was the door to her bedroom, closed. In the left corner of her living room was her exercise equipment. On the right, her father's old desk with work piled on it. Everything on the surface

48

was open to the world. Delve any deeper and what would he get? A closed door.

"I need to talk to you," said Mason in earnest.

"I don't have anything to say to you."

"Good. I don't want you to say anything. I just want you to listen." He smiled at her like he was trying to ignite some of the camaraderie they shared. "Look, just give me the amount of time it takes me to fix your door."

Cara walked away but she returned moments later with tools. "Talk."

"Monahan told me you took all the time you had coming to you." Cara opened her mouth to speak. "Don't say anything, Cara. I don't think I could take it if you lied to me." He looked up at her from the floor. She turned away and went to sit on the couch, feeling him follow her with his eyes. "I've had some time to think about it since we had our blowout, and I know that if I were in your shoes I would do what you're doing. What I came here to say is that I want to help. You tell me what you need, and I'll get it. It won't be official, but we can find the guy. If it has nothing to do with Dizzazio, we can go ahead and prosecute. If it does, then we'll still have the evidence; we'll just have to wait until Dizzazio goes to trial."

Cara narrowed her eyes. *Is he playing me?* She risked a peek. Honesty and hurt was the only thing she was getting from him. They had never been as close as she and Danny were. They were friends though, and she knew that Mason took friendship seriously. He didn't have many either.

"Thank you, Mason. I know you mean what you say, but I can't accept your help. If you get caught it's your career. I'm not even sure I want to go back, so my job is expendable; yours is not."

"You need someone on the inside. You can't get to the information I can from out here."

"I have a source of information. You can't help me, Mason."

"Cara, I'm warning you, if you go off on your own you're going to get hurt. If you don't let me help you with this, I'll take you in."

"For what?"

"You are the only one who can give a description of Christian Black. So far I'm the only one that knows that, but if you push me I'll let the cat out of the bag. I only need you to sit with a sketch artist but I'll tie you up in protective custody for months before I let you go out on your own. By the time you get out, the trail will be ice cold."

Cara stared at him. *He would do it, too. Men stink.* "I can't tell you, Mason. There is so much more at stake here than just your job."

"What, my life? That's on the line every day. I'm a cop remember?"

"You wouldn't believe me if I told you."

"Try me."

She did.

"You need a vacation," was his reply to her story.

She grabbed his hand and read his mind. "I didn't hit my head."

He snatched his hand back. "Lucky guess."

"Okay," she smiled. "Think of something no one else knows. Something I couldn't guess." He looked reluctant and unease was coming off of him in waves. He held out his hand. Cara took it, looked him in the eye, and said, "You're a grounder."

This time he flung her hand away from his and jumped up from the couch. "Shit! Here I thought you were so normal." He threw the accusation at her.

Cara knew what a grounder was because of Beth. She also knew what it was like to have something you didn't want. She was still insulted. "Don't you dare, Mason. You bullied your way in here demanding the truth. Now you have it. If you don't want any part of me, fine, leave. I didn't want you involved to begin with, but don't talk to me like I'm some kind of freak."

Mason ran a frustrated hand through his hair. "I'm sorry. I didn't mean it that way. My whole life I stayed away from the whole 'other world' bit. I never liked the idea that there were things I couldn't explain. Now you're telling me that Danny was killed by a vampire. I think I'm entitled to go overboard."

"Look, why don't you go home. It's late and I still have something I want to go do." She walked to the door.

"I didn't like the idea of you going up against a hired assassin. You think I'm going to let you take on vampires by yourself? Besides, I told you I don't like the other world. I could probably stand to take out a few. And we are not going anywhere tonight. I'm staying here and we can go out at first light if you want." His expression said *no arguments*.

"Fine. I'm tired of arguing with everyone. But not at first light. Beth will kill me if I get to her house at the crack of dawn. Finish my lock."

"I have no idea how to put that thing back together."

They looked at each other for a moment and then burst out laughing. After calling a locksmith, which at this time of night cost her a fortune, they sat at the dining room table to go over everything again.

She told him everything she knew—well, almost everything. For some reason, she could not bring herself to mention the kiss she had shared with Jonathan or the item snug in her pocket. Finally when the door was again secure and Mason's head could handle no more thoughts about the paranormal, Cara made up the couch for him and retreated to her bedroom.

CHAPTER 11

Jonathan stared at the door Cara had just shut in his face and wanted to smash it. She had gone right for the throat. He couldn't blame her for being upset. Everything that had been thrown at her over the last couple of days would put anyone out. That didn't stop him from feeling as if her words had physically hit him. How had this happened? She wasn't supposed to mean anything to him. He went back down to his car and sat there. It was nine o'clock. He would keep watch over her until morning, and then Thomas could take over. He phoned him and told him his plan to watch her apartment.

The lights were on, so he could see her shadow move behind the shades. She appeared to be getting ready to leave when his attention was brought back down to the street. A man parked next to her building and got out of his car. He scanned the street as if making sure there was no one there. From the practiced way he surveyed the area, it was obvious that he was used to doing this kind of thing. Despite the suspicious behavior, Jonathan did not sense any immediate danger and decided to watch closely, but from a reasonable distance.

When the man entered Cara's building, Jonathan got out of his car and followed. He stayed behind until the man reached Cara's apartment. When the visitor looked at the door, he noticed something was amiss. Jonathan could tell that this was no amateur as he pushed the door open gently and peered inside.

Jonathan heard the man ask what had happened to her door and heard her reply. Obviously this was someone she knew. Jonathan went calmly back down to his car and returned his attention to the window. They were talking. Cara moved out of sight for a moment and returned. They both went in the direction of the front door, but after a few moments neither had left the building. Just as Jonathan was about to go up, the shadowy forms of Cara and the stranger came back into sight. As they sat on the couch they were out of his line of vision.

Jonathan was sitting there quietly when the shadow couple leapt from the sofa, and Jonathan poised himself to fly up, literally. The larger silhouette walked toward the smaller one. They didn't touch but they were close. Then they both disappeared. An hour later a locksmith arrived. Jonathan breathed a bit freer; even though he was keeping watch, he did not like the idea that the lock on Cara's front door was absolutely useless.

An hour later, the lights in the apartment went out. The stranger hadn't left. Shortly after that, Jonathan ripped the steering wheel off of his car.

CHAPTER 12

Thomas didn't ask any questions when he was asked to have a rental car delivered to Jonathan in the wee hours of the morning. When he relieved him a few hours later, he was tempted to laugh, but he didn't relish having his face rearranged. Thomas took his post as Jonathan screeched off into the gathering light of the coming dawn. At nine o'clock Thomas tailed Cara and her visitor to a diner. They had breakfast, he didn't. Then they drove west to a dirt road that seemed to wind forever. Lord help him if this was some kind of love nest. He wasn't sure he had the courage to face Jonathan with that bit of news.

Soon he saw a house in the distance and pulled his car to the side. Hiding it as best he could, he peered through the trees and saw what every good horror story needed, a gothic-style one-story with gargoyles on each corner. *What the hell?*

The front door opened and Thomas' jaw hit the ground. A young girl? She was a tiny woman with straight blonde hair that reached her waist as she bounced onto the doorstep. A very large black dog sat patiently at her feet. She seemed excited to see the visitors but didn't rush out to greet them, hopping up and down until they reached her. She ushered them in, and just before she shut the door she popped her head out. She looked right in his direction and he could swear he saw her wink. *No way!* She couldn't have seen him. He went back to his car and waited for his shift to be over.

Beth closed the door. Cara knew she was so happy to have visitors—it got very lonely way out there.

"What took you so long? I've been expecting you for the last couple days. Are you okay? How's the investigation? I wish you had told me you were going to bring someone, I would have cleaned up a bit more. Not too much more, mind you, but at least a bit. Did you know there was someone outside? I think he followed you. He doesn't mean any harm, but I thought you should know. What is that positively icky thing in your pocket? Well, are you going to introduce us?" As the words flew out of Beth's mouth she whipped around the kitchen making coffee.

Cara smiled at her friend and spoke up, "Beth, this is Mason. He works at the department with me. Mason, this is Beth, resident whirlwind. Yes, I know there is someone following us. His name is Thomas. The investigation has hit a few snags." Cara chewed on her lower lip. She hated to involve Beth in something this dangerous, but Beth could help her in a way no one else could.

"Should we invite him in?" Beth asked.

"No, let him sit there." Cara replied.

"Nice to meet you, Beth." Mason looked over at the sprite in front of him. She was several inches shorter than Cara, which made her a scant five feet. Her long blonde hair fell to her waist, and she had the most unusual eyes. They were violet and seemed to twinkle in complete harmony with the dimples that marked her face when she smiled. Beth was the complete opposite of Cara. She was rounded where Cara was slim.

"Look, Cara, he can't decide which one of us is cuter. Let me help, it's me!" She laughed, but Mason wasn't amused.

"You're psychic too?" He looked ready to run to the door.

"No, of course not. It was written all over your face. Wait, what do you mean *too*?" She looked directly at Cara. "It came back?"

"And a whole lot more." Cara sat at the large wood table in Beth's dining room. "Grab your soda and come sit down. This is going to take awhile."

Beth went to the kitchen.

"Nice dog." As soon as Mason said that, the animal growled at him, and the police officer stepped back.

"She's a wolf. Her name is Sheena." Beth sat at the table quietly in a sudden change of pace, as if the hurricane had suddenly chosen to reveal its tranquil eye.

Cara began to relay all that had happened over the last week. She paused and glanced at Mason who sat up straight in his chair.

"What?"

"When Danny was murdered…" Cara stopped again. Not only was she hesitant to mention the object she lifted from the scene but the simple fact that she had disturbed the scene would surely upset Mason. Cara was uncertain which would put him out more.

"Keep going." Mason braced himself to his chair.

Beth became still as well, as though sensing something bad was coming.

"I don't even know why I took it. I just knew I couldn't leave it there."

"Took what?" Mason pressed. "You took something from the murder site?! Are you crazy?!"

Cara sighed, reached into her pocket, pulled out the object and dropped it on the table.

Beth gasped and shoved her chair back from the table. Covering her ears with her hands, she ran for the library.

Mason's face went white and he bolted for the bathroom. At the sound of Mason's retching Cara had to assume the object bothered him more.

Cara didn't move, she just glared at the hunk of metal on the table. Obviously it had more of an impact on Mason and Beth. Why not her? Beth returned with a small iron chest and a camera.

She snapped pictures rapidly, muttered a 'yuck' as she plucked the thing from the table and dropped it in the chest. Slamming the lid Beth locked it with magic.

Lock this box
Right and tight
Not to be opened
By will or might
Hide it well
From prying eyes
Invisible from
Earth to skies

White light formed in the palm of Beth's hand and drifted down to surround the chest, glowing brightly for a moment then absorbing into it. Beth continued to stare at it a moment.

"It doesn't like being hidden away." When Cara opened her mouth to speak Beth held up a hand. "Don't ask yet. Let me print these." Beth took the digital camera and went back to the library. The bathroom door opened and Mason walked out slowly.

"Where is it?" he asked and Cara pointed to the chest. "God Cara, how could you stand to touch that thing?"

"I don't know."

"I do," Beth yelled from the library. "I'm almost done."

"I can't believe you disturbed a crime scene." Mason paced and kept shooting the chest uneasy looks.

"So I should have left it there?"

"No. I guess not, but you could have said something last night."

"Look what just happened. I had to wait."

"Okay, let's see what we have here." Beth came in with her hands full of pictures. She sat down and Mason joined them. Beth handed them each several photos. Mason hesitated to touch even the images, but finally pulled one to him sighing with relief when nothing happened.

"It's a lump of metal." Mason tossed the picture back on the table. Cara was still unsure of why it made him ill.

"It's a dragon head." Cara guessed.

"Don't quit your day jobs." Beth looked at both of them with pity in her eyes. "It used to be a ring. Of a man with rubies for eyes and fanged teeth."

Cara turned the photos to different angles and Mason followed her lead. She felt skeptical and Mason shrugged and tossed the pictures back to the table.

"Trust me, this is what I do." Beth gathered the photos together.

"I know. So tell me why this thing only tickled your gross factor but it made Mason hurl?"

"Hey!" Mason kicked her chair.

"Sorry Mas."

"Well, Mason, what are your talents? I see several things going on like you're undecided." Beth leaned forward taking a closer look at him.

"I don't know what you mean." Mason was shifting in his seat under Beth's scrutiny.

"Come on. All that power is swirling around in you. What can you do with it?"

Cara smiled as Mason perked up at the mention of power.

"Well, technically, I guess I'm uh, a grounder."

Cara found it interesting that Mason could swear like a sailor and dodge bullets on a daily basis but whispered "grounder" like he was a small boy being forced to rat out his friends.

"There's more Mason, I'm not sure what, but there's much more to you," Beth smiled.

Mason blew out a pent up breath that seemed to say he was afraid of that.

CHAPTER 13

Beth moved about the kitchen preparing lunch. Even with all that Cara had revealed, Beth knew when Cara left something out. She didn't feel slighted; she would fill in those gaps. She watched as Mason chose to explore her house, all the while keeping a safe distance from Sheena.

"So you want to tell me that one little thing you left out?" Beth could hardly wait. Even in the face of danger her enthusiasm and quest for knowledge didn't wane.

Cara cast a glance over her shoulder for Mason, then quietly told Beth about the kiss. "It was so stupid, Beth. I only knew the man for two days." Cara was clearly disgusted with herself.

"It sounds wonderful to me. You don't find that kind of chemistry every day." Cara gave her a bland expression, and Beth quickly followed up, "Okay, I see what you mean, he's a vampire. But he's a cute vampire, and a good one."

Cara stared back at her. Beth had always been so accepting of everything. Of course, she had to be. She had a bright outlook on life. "Oh, sure. He's a vampire. No big deal." Cara went back to making sandwiches.

"Do you think we should invite our other guest in? I think it's about time." Beth looked out her kitchen window and cocked her head to the side. "We'll have to later anyway."

Cara looked at Beth and nodded.

Beth went to Mason and asked him to go get Thomas and bring him in. He looked like it was the last thing on earth he wanted to do but saw her smiling and couldn't say no.

Mason marched down the lane and neared the car. It was only half hidden by the foliage. By the time he made it there, Thomas was out and standing beside it.

"You're wanted inside." Mason's tone was intended to say that it certainly wasn't him that wanted Thomas there.

"Why?"

"Lunch."

CHAPTER 14

The little woman, and it was a woman, was standing on the doorstep. She wasn't as happy to see Thomas as she was Cara and the other guy, but she gave him a brilliant smile nonetheless. As he got closer, she frowned and her eyes narrowed on him; the animal at her feet snarled. *Can't be a wolf or can it?* he thought to himself. Beth put a hand down and quieted the animal. Thomas began to get uncomfortable until she shrugged and smiled once more.

"Hi," Beth moved back and let him pass. She shivered when he went by, and Thomas stopped and looked at her quizzically. "I'm Beth. I can't wait to hear what you have to say on all this, but let's get you some nourishment first." She showed him to the dining room and sat him at the table. He glanced at the iron chest but dismissed it as décor.

"Gee, what a surprise," Cara said wryly.

"He doesn't mean any harm," Beth attested, shocking Thomas.

Cara seemed to take Beth's remark more seriously than when Jonathan had tried to tell her the same thing.

"Okay, but any more breaking down doors or probing where you're not wanted, and you're history," Cara said.

"I take it these two know," was Thomas' reply.

"Yes, these are people I trust." Cara stared at him with no apology. Thomas watched Beth as he ate. She was taking all of this very well. In fact she seemed downright thrilled. She was also gorgeous. Those eyes were incredible. Though short, she had a very shapely figure and Thomas had always liked curves. She caught him staring and smiled at him.

"See, Cara, even Thomas thinks *I'm* the cute one," she said smiling.

Thomas blushed. "Are you like her?" Thomas gestured his head toward Cara.

"No," was all she said.

After lunch Thomas and Beth went to her library. It turned out to be a huge room off of the living room with wall-to-wall books. In the midst of the beautifully crafted bookcases that lined each wall, several long tables were scattered with all types of relics, masks, talismans, and similar strange-looking devices.

Beth must have seen the face Thomas was giving her because she sought to reassure him. "Don't worry. I freelance consult for museums and such. They send artifacts to me, and I tell them how old they are, where they come from, and stuff like that."

"What about all the books?" He was genuinely interested.

"Some are points of reference, and some I use for translations of old texts. Others are just good company." She gazed at her library.

"How are these going to help us?"

"Some of these books are filled with folklore and legends. There's bound to be something that will help."

"Legends are going to help us?"

"You would be surprised how many times I have found that folklore closely parallels the truth."

"Where do we start?"

Beth, Cara and Thomas settled in the library and spent hours pouring over Beth's books. Thomas felt his eyes starting to cross. There did seem to be some truth in them, but nothing that would help them with this particular brand of evil. He sat back and rubbed his eyes. His gaze turned to Beth and Cara. He felt like he was spinning his wheels until he could contact Jonathan but for now he was exactly where he was supposed to be.

He was beginning to like Cara, but every time he looked at Beth— *Zap!* He couldn't get over how different the two women were, and that went way beyond the physical. Cara was so still that you had to wonder if she was even breathing sometimes, but Beth was in constant motion. Her toes tapped the floor and her fingers beat a tempo on the table. He could see how close they were, an almost visible energy flowed between them.

Mason had commandeered the use of Beth's phone. His network of men were throwing a virtual blanket over Miami. While Cara, Beth, and Thomas tried to find a way to rid themselves of Christian without putting any of them in harm's way, Mason was trying to find him. He spent an hour on the phone giving Barry instructions on looking up recent unsolved homicides. Vampires had to feed, maybe they didn't like to go far from home to do it, he had said. He then contacted the rest of his team to give them a head's up. He didn't reveal exactly what was going on, but he let them know that they needed to watch their backs more closely and that the stakes had just been raised. *Pardon the pun,* Thomas thought. Mason finally detached the phone from his ear and looked up at the others.

He still looked as though he expected one of the artifacts to attack or the books to begin flinging themselves from the shelves. Beth went to the corner and pulled out a fairly new volume, then walked back to Mason and handed it to him.

"Here, look through this one, it might help."

Thomas stood and looked at the book in Mason's hand. *"Grounding."*

Cara watched their exchange for a moment, then joined them in the corner. Mason's expression was akin to someone holding a rattler; afraid to hold it, but afraid of what might happen if he let it go.

"I know what you're thinking," Cara said to him. Thomas watched as Mason's color darkened. "All my life I've been pretending my ability would go away, like some dreaded disease. It didn't, although it changed from what I believe it was originally supposed to be because of the will I placed over it. Mason, look what we're faced with. Isn't it in our own best interest to explore all our options and fight with whatever power we can muster?"

"Grounding is a witch's tool for spells. It won't work here." Mason looked ready to run.

"In recent years grounders have tapped into more uses for their abilities than simply assisting in spells." Beth was practically pleading with the guy.

Mason tucked the book under his arm.

"Something you'd like to share?" Thomas eyed them all, lingering on Beth.

"No." Thomas had no idea why, but his very presence seemed to put Mason on edge.

"It's personal," Beth said quietly, her violet eyes holding Thomas'.

"I don't think we have time for personal," spit back Thomas. "If it's important enough for the three of you to confer over, maybe it should be shared."

"Okay," Beth smiled up at him, "you first. We don't have every detail about you. But then, maybe not all secrets should be told, am I right?"

"Point taken."

Cara took the book she was studying and followed Mason with his to the living room. Thomas closely trailed Beth to the kitchen.

"Do you know my secret?" Thomas felt he was tense and tried to relax.

"No. We all have at least one though. One we don't share with everyone. I can tell you have one. It's written all over you, or rather it's not." She was gazing at him again; studying him from head to foot.

"What do you mean, not?" Thomas leaned against the counter, more relieved.

"Oh, never mind." She waved a dainty hand at him and turned to the refrigerator. He watched her move around the kitchen and thought he understood how Jonathan could have been instantly drawn to Cara.

"I hope you'll let me in on at least a few of your secrets. I would really like to take you out when this is over." The words popped out of his mouth without a thought.

"I don't go out," Beth said just loud enough for him to hear; she still had her back to him. "However, you could come here and I could make us dinner."

"I could do that."

Beth turned and gave him a brilliant smile. "Don't look too happy. Tonight you have to help cook." Beth handed Thomas a bag of potatoes, pointed to the sink, and ordered him to peel. At this point, he would have done nearly anything she wanted.

Beth filled a pot with water and turned toward the stove. As Thomas watched, she stopped short and tilted her head to the side as if she were listening for something that no one else could hear. Suddenly she gasped and doubled over, wrapping her arms around her waist and dropping the pot of tap-warm water which hit the floor and splashed everywhere. Thomas immediately leapt to her side, bringing her against him, focusing all his senses on her in an attempt to understand what was happening. He gave a glance at the wolf, which ran to the door snarling.

"What? What's wrong?" His gut knotted with tension as he waited for her to speak.

When she did, it was but a whisper. "They're coming."

CHAPTER 15

"They're out by the first turnoff. I can't tell how many." Beth turned to face Thomas and grabbed the front of his shirt. "Evil, Thomas, they're evil through and through."

Thomas didn't stop to ask how Beth knew what she was telling him. He yelled for Cara and Mason. As he explained what she had said, he grabbed the phone and relayed the same information to Jonathan along with their location. Just before he said good-bye, the line went dead.

Thomas looked at Mason, who was drawing his gun and peering out through the window. "A dozen or so in the trees." The detective's voice was clipped. "Shit, we should have noticed the sun was down."

"Wait, there's something else out there." Thomas blinked to be sure his eyes weren't playing tricks on him. "They're flying," he whispered.

"Those are gargoyles." Beth said it as if that explained everything. Thomas saw Mason's blank expression and knew it mirrored his own.

"They live here, but there's only two and once they have their prey they won't come back until—" she paused.

"Until what?" Thomas knew he should be focused on the coming battle but couldn't tear his gaze from Beth as she struggled with the answer.

"Um, well they won't return until they're full."

"Full," Thomas repeated. As if on cue a scream went up and Thomas watched as one of the gargoyles grabbed a vampire with its front claws and threw him to the ground. The vampire battled uselessly as the gargoyle batted his prize back to the ground, stepped on him and clutched him with the talons on its feet. With a mighty sweep of wings, the gargoyle launched into the sky with its still struggling dinner. Silence prevailed until the second gargoyle made his choice, created a slightly bigger mess of his meal and flew away.

"Okay, okay," Thomas said to himself.

"Yeah, just keep saying that and maybe it will come true," Mason muttered.

Thomas went to the library and returned with a sword Beth had been analyzing for a museum. He took a position by the front door and spoke quietly to Mason, "When they come in, shoot them in the heart. It won't kill them, but it will slow them down enough for me to cut their heads off." Mason nodded and shoved an extra clip in his front pocket. Cara and Beth hadn't moved, but an understanding look passed between them just as Thomas glanced in their direction.

"What now?" Thomas had the impression he wasn't going to like the answer.

"They can't get through the door. It's protected." Beth stepped forward.

"Protected by what?" Thomas went very still.

"A spell," came Beth's quiet reply.

"A spell? As in a witch's spell? You're a witch!" Thomas felt as if someone had just kicked him in the balls. He glanced at Mason, who seemed equally as surprised and suddenly wary. *At least I'm not the only asshole here.*

The front door burst open, splintering the frame. A vampire stood with teeth bared a scant two feet from the door. He snarled and made a running start for the door, but the instant his foot hit the threshold, he flew backwards through the air and landed in the dirt. Two more followed, with the same results. They began circling the house like they were searching for a weakness.

Thomas looked at Beth: she had her eyes closed and perspiration dotted her forehead. Her arms were away from her body with her palms up, and a fuzzy white glow surrounded her entire body.

"What's she doing?" He couldn't help but take a step away from her.

"She's reinforcing the spell. It wasn't set to keep anything that powerful out. It's really only to warn her when someone approaches."

Thomas inwardly seethed. It finally occurred to him that he hadn't even thought to ask how she knew anyone was coming.

"Can you help her, Mason?" Cara looked Mason in the eye as if trying to will him to do it.

"I don't know. I have never done anything like that before." He walked slowly to Beth and stood in front of her, unsure how to proceed. He looked back at Cara and Thomas.

Thomas could see that Beth was struggling, her breathing had become labored, the glow that had surrounded her was now but a halo around her head, and her whole body trembled. *She's going to fly apart.* The pack could be heard battering the house, and rocks began to fly through the windows.

"Please, Mason, you have to try!" Cara seemed to be close to tears.

"It can't be any worse than taking on a pack of vampires that want to suck the life out of me." He put his gun in the waistband of his jeans and stood facing Beth. For another moment he seemed uncertain, then he slid his hands into her open palms. Her eyes never opened, but instantly her fingers laced with his. He tilted his head up and closed his eyes, copying her posture.

Beth inhaled, sounding as though she were taking a long-awaited breath. The halo grew to encompass their whole bodies, and instead of fuzzy it turned to bright white. Thomas watched them and found the intimacy of the rite bothered him. *Witch, witch, witch. He can have her.* The thought didn't comfort him.

The pack had sensed the weakness of the spell and redoubled their efforts to invade. Now silence descended. Thomas saw Beth hold her breath. He looked out through the shattered windows and saw the pack approaching. Thomas whipped his head back to Mason and Beth, the power still shimmered around them. He looked at Cara in confusion.

"Don't move," she commanded when Thomas looked as if he

would venture outside and fight. Shadows reached the front door and windows as the attackers began to will themselves into the house. Beth gripped Mason's hand so hard that her knuckles turned white. Suddenly a light burst from between them, so purely white and bright that Thomas and Cara threw their arms up to protect their eyes. The light split into ten separate beams that zeroed in like lightning on their targets. As each beam made contact it propelled an invader back out of the house, searing its body until the entire pack burst into flames and fell to the ground, rolling and flailing about in an effort to extinguish themselves.

Beth released Mason and fell to the floor.

"The fire won't kill them. Mason, same plan! Let's move!" Thomas darted out through the door. Mason followed, stumbling down the first steps, but catching himself.

Thomas looked behind him and saw Cara exiting the house with gun in hand. Even Sheena was getting into the action, darting through the doorway and attacking the first intruder she came to. She tore into his throat and went for another. She was fury in motion, muscles bunching and straining.

Thomas headed towards the ones who were putting their flames out. Mason shot each one in the heart, and Thomas lopped off their heads. Cara kept an eye on the surroundings. Mason changed the clip in his gun and turned to shoot one of the last of them when a charred body flew out of the trees and tackled him. Landing on his back he threw both hands up to keep the fanged creature from biting him.

Cara appeared over its shoulder and shot it in the back. Its head reared up as it howled in agony, and Thomas swung his sword in a savage arc, slicing it off in one clean, powerful sweep. Cara had to duck as the head flew toward her with the follow through of the sword's movement.

Mason pushed the decapitated body off of him and scrambled to his feet.

"I don't think I like having heads lobbed at me," Cara said.

Thomas and Mason cracked a smile, then started laughing.

When Jonathan drove in that was precisely how he found them; standing beside a windowless house, in a yard littered with heads separated from blackened bodies, covered in blood and laughing. Thomas had his arm slung around Cara's shoulders as if they were old friends.

Cara saw Jonathan first and got all serious as though trying to recover.

"What is going on?" Jonathan looked from one to the other.

"Nothing," Thomas grinned.

Jonathan raised an eyebrow at that, but his reply was cut off by the look on Mason's face, a look that Thomas read easily: he'd like to get in one more vampire.

Thomas sobered and drew back from Cara when he saw Beth at the front door. She looked okay, but not as energetic as before.

"I take it he's the good one," Beth said smiling.

"Depends on your definition of good," Mason said and stomped away from the house towards Cara's car.

CHAPTER 16

They took turns cleaning up and filling Jonathan in. For one reason or another they were all used to being prepared for anything and each had a change of clothes. Beth had plenty of plywood to cover the windows and they made repairs quickly, knowing that they still had a lot to discuss and to plan for. Mason finished changing and followed Jonathan to the kitchen. After the gusto with which Sheena went after the bad guys Mason fed her anything she wanted from the fridge.

"What about the bodies?" Beth obviously wasn't thrilled with the idea of all the corpses lying in her yard.

"The sunlight will take care of them," Jonathan said nonchalantly.

"You're just going to leave them there for the rest of the night?" Beth shifted uneasily.

"Fine, I'll have someone take care of them." Jonathan reached for the phone he had reconnected. He liked Beth. How could he not when she had accepted him so easily.

"I thought only removing the heart or sunlight truly killed a vampire. Is there a chance these might come back somehow?" Beth asked.

"Well, someone would first have to reunite the heads with the bodies. Unless you're going to run out and give them a hand, we shouldn't have anything to worry about." He was smiling and teasing her. She rolled her eyes, waved a hand at him, and walked into the kitchen. He saw Thomas glare at her back.

Later, cleaned up and refueled with caffeine, they sat at the kitchen table to discuss how to proceed.

71

"I think we should all go our separate ways," Thomas said. "Jonathan and I can do what we do, and you three can continue with the hocus pocus."

Beth's jaw dropped.

"Fine by me," said Mason. "See ya."

"What do you mean, hocus pocus?" Beth asked, her chin set at a defensive angle.

"I mean, you're a witch. I mean, who knows what you're hiding under that lovely spell. Witches are untrustworthy and cruel and I have no intention of working with one." His voice was a growl.

Beth seemed to shrink into her seat and the color drained from her face. Jonathan could see Cara and Mason about to go on the attack and rose to put a hand on Thomas' arm.

"Don't, Jonathan," Thomas turned to him. "You can ask anything, anything of me, but not this."

Mason rose and stood between Thomas and Beth. "So we're supposed to accept the walking dead over here at face value, but it doesn't go both ways?"

"Suits me just fine. I'd rather have Jonathan at my back than spooky over there. She'd probably put a knife in it."

Mason swung and connected, sending Thomas reeling to the ground. "Seems to me that she covered your ass pretty well a little while ago."

Cara had rushed around the table and now held Mason back, barely. Thomas got up, and Jonathan held him in check. It didn't take much.

"You know everything about my past, Thomas," Cara's voice was quiet. "It was Beth who brought me out. She was the only one who could have. If she hadn't, I would still be trapped inside my own suffering and that little girl's. Is that someone cruel? You have no idea how much she suffered because of that. She—"

"No," Beth rose and stood in front of Thomas, interrupting Cara as she did so. "You don't need to explain for me." She looked Thomas in the eye and he turned away from her. They stood grid locked; everyone thinking, no one speaking.

Jonathan broke the silence, "I think we can all agree that our best bet is to work together. He's coming after all of us now."

With that, Thomas turned and looked back at Beth. Jonathan's eyes looked over at her pale face, even the color of her eyes seemed to have faded.

"Okay. We've established that we are unwilling partners. Maybe we should split up." Cara's training was taking over. "We'll make Beth's house the base of our operations. We'll split up and do what we each do best, checking in with Beth every two hours. Beth can disseminate any information we need and from here she can also continue her research."

"I don't know how much more I can find." Beth seemed on an even keel again. "There are several mentions of a tome in my older texts; a vampire manual of sorts, but, there's only one. It can't be copied or held by mortal hands, unless a vampire willingly gives it to them. It's protected by powerful magic. Vampires have their own kind of witchcraft." Jonathan caught her as she flashed a condescending look at Thomas. "Even if we were able to find it, I doubt it would be handed over willingly. But if we could get our hands on that work somehow, there just might be a chance that it would give us the clue we need."

"I'll check out any information that Barry has pulled up," said Cara.

"You're not on the force anymore," Mason chimed in. "I'll have to get it for you. I'll check in with my men while I'm at it."

Thomas shook his head at Jonathan who watched Cara's expression as she witnessed it.

"What?" she demanded. "You're so keen on knowing everyone's secrets. Share yours."

Jonathan took a deep breath and said, "It's not his to tell. I have the book Beth spoke of."

Beth perked up immediately. Whether it was the thought of holding a book that would probably be older than anything she'd ever seen, or the fact that it may help them, wasn't clear.

"Why didn't you say so?"

"He didn't say so because he's not about to put in our hands what could destroy him." Mason said it like throwing out a challenge.

"To be honest," Jonathan gritted his teeth wondering if they would all kill each other before Christian could get to them. "I didn't bring it up because I've studied it for years, and I'm convinced that nothing in it can help us with this." He got up and paced the room. "It's written in many different languages, some I can't even locate. I spent two centuries trying to translate it." He glanced at Cara. She had an odd look on her face. He realized he had caught her staring at him, watching his movements, but she didn't look away, and the room began to heat.

"Maybe you just didn't look in the right place. Jonathan, at least let me try." Beth looked like a little girl waiting for a piece of candy.

Thomas leaned close to Beth. "No witch can resist the lure of more power."

Cara and Mason rose simultaneously from their seats, but Beth put a hand, palm out, to stop them. Then she shifted her hand to face Thomas. A small, unseen, electric current shot from her hand and hit Thomas square in the chest, flipping him back out of his chair. Jonathan started for Beth when he heard a laugh. He turned to see Cara with her hand over her mouth.

"She used to do that to boys who got too, uh, fresh. They never could figure out what happened." When she saw the angry look on Thomas' face she sobered.

"She's laughing. That witch electrocuted me, and she's laughing." Thomas was sitting in the middle of the floor.

"I am a witch. I wouldn't change it even if I could. I don't expect you to believe that I'm also a good *human* being." The emphasis she put on the word had Jonathan looking at Thomas. Jonathan merely shrugged. "You can have the decency not to treat me like a rabid dog in my own home. I've never hurt you; in fact, Mason's right, I did protect you, and even after all you've said I would do it again." Beth's voice trembled as she finished, and she held out her hand in peace and forgiveness. Thomas looked at her small white hand and ignored it, getting to his feet on his own. Jonathan saw the disappointment pass over her. He'd always heard that witches couldn't cry, but he saw Beth's eyes fill and the tears roll down her face. She turned and looked at Cara. Their mysterious link caught and held, and Cara looked as if she were in pain too. Beth left the room and closed herself in the library.

"Thomas!" Cara's voice was low and dangerous. She crossed to the room to stand directly in front of him, Mason at her back. The air simmered around her. "She is not like the rest of us, and I'm not talking about being a witch. She is something apart from us mere mortals, and this will be the only warning you'll ever get. Hurt her again and I'll kill you."

Thomas held her stare and Jonathan saw that he believed her.

"If this keeps up we might as well save Christian the trouble," Jonathan said, voicing his earlier thoughts. "Truce on all counts until this is over." It really wasn't a request.

"I'll back off," Thomas said quietly, staring at the closed library door.

They all seemed much more drained from fighting with each other than they had been from combating their earlier evils. Mason got ready to leave to make his rounds. He would be taking Cara's car, so she walked him out, discussing exactly what he planned to say to the other officers.

Jonathan stayed back waiting for Thomas to speak.

"Shit. What a mess!" Thomas rubbed his hands over his face.

"Eloquently put! I know how you feel about witches, but she's different and I think you can see that." Thomas didn't reply. "Go check in with our own men. I'm taking Cara to her apartment to pick up some things so she can stay here. Then we'll go back to my place. She'll be taking my car, so I'll need you to pick me up tomorrow evening—or tonight." He corrected himself after glancing at his watch. It was only a couple more hours to sunrise.

"Did you tell Cara about me?" Thomas asked cautiously.

"No. I didn't think you had to ask." Jonathan was taken aback.

"I didn't think so, but Beth knew. I could tell. You noticed that little inflection on the word *human* didn't you?" Thomas looked toward the library door, it was still firmly shut.

"I noticed." Jonathan held his tongue as Cara walked back in.

"While we're sharing," Beth returned with the photos of the hunk of metal tucked safely in the box and handed them to Jonathan.

What's this?" Jonathan took the pictures. His hand tightened on the photos. "This is Christian's. How did you get pictures of it?"

"We have it." Beth never took her gaze from Jonathan.

"What...?" Jonathan whispered almost to himself. It wasn't a question, more like sheer disbelief. "Where? How?" Jonathan felt himself becoming more agitated.

"I took it," Cara said.

"It's in there," Beth pointed to the chest.

"Oh my God. You have to get it out of here." Jonathan reached for it but Beth stayed him.

"It's okay."

"No, no. You don't understand. I never saw him without it. I did see him kill a lover he'd been with for two decades because she kept asking to wear it. It made me sick to be near it, near him."

"You're not the only one," Mason muttered as his phone rang, and he excused himself.

"You don't feel it now, do you?" Beth asked.

"No, and apparently Cara had it and I didn't sense it." Jonathan looked at Cara, accusation flooding from him.

"Cara's abilities are growing, but she's always been adept at blocking."

"He's going to want this back. He's going to come after it."

"He already has," Mason said as he snapped his phone shut.

CHAPTER 17

According to the news, the attack on the station was swift, brutal. While the group at Beth's was fighting for their lives, the officers at the station fought for their own. Security cameras caught nothing but strange blurs before they were destroyed. The officers looked like they had no time to call for help or to help themselves. Weapons were still holstered and the armory untouched. The evidence room was destroyed. They had no leads at this time but they suspected a group of individuals were trying to make a point by attacking the police on their own turf.

"The entire city is on the edge of panic tonight. If the police can't protect themselves how will they be able to protect us? This is Shelly Martin reporting."

Beth jabbed the power button on the TV. "She should be ashamed of herself," said Beth tossing the remote down.

"She's a reporter, they don't do shame." Cara paced.

"Mason's back." Beth went to the door and opened it for him.

He looked beaten, defeated. He didn't sit, but drifted to the kitchen, opened the fridge and shut it, bracing his hands on the door.

"I *know* who did this and I can't tell anyone what happened or what they're looking for. Do you have any idea how I felt watching everyone scurry around trying to figure out what was happening while I have all the answers they're killing themselves to find. I was helpless and useless." Mason pushed away from the fridge.

Beth came behind him, and placed a hand on his back. "This isn't your fault. We'll find a way."

"Yeah, well we better find it soon and we better be sure Christian doesn't get what he wants."

"What are you saying, Mas?" Cara moved closer.

"I managed to grab part of the video feed from the station. There's no visual but I heard voices. I couldn't make everything out, so... I took it. Me, I *stole* evidence. Anyway, I stopped at an outside source and he cleaned it for me. You can listen for yourself but its Christian having an absolute shit fit. He's screaming at his men to find that fucking piece of shit that you can't even tell what the fuck it is!" Mason was yelling now clenching and unclenching his fists. "He says he needs it for the ascension. He says he's waited 300 years and he'll tear through the city if he has to. While he was saying all this he was ripping through those men like they were nothing. If you want to hear I'll be in the other room." Mason threw the disc on the kitchen table and left the room.

"Oh, God." Beth covered her face with her hands. "Jonathan, what is the ascension?"

"I have no idea but it might be in the book in one of the languages I can't translate. I'll leave as soon as the sun goes down. Until then we might want to get some rest."

CHAPTER 18

As soon as the sun set Mason left for the station. He hadn't said much to anyone and still looked as if the world rested on his shoulders. He and Cara made arrangements to meet later. Thomas left for face to face meetings with the men hired to look out for vampire activity. Jonathan and Cara left for Jonathan's apartment and the silence was tense.

"Maybe Thomas is right. I don't know if this is going to work." Jonathan finally broke the quiet in the car. They were almost to her apartment and neither had spoken.

"I'm not altogether sure that Thomas wouldn't just offer up Beth to Christian. The only reason he hasn't is that he knows you would never forgive him." She slid him a look out of the corner of her eye.

Jonathan pulled to a stop in front of her building, putting more pressure on the brake than was necessary. "Two things we need to get straight: I don't have a problem with Beth, and Thomas wouldn't do that, even to a witch. I don't want to argue with you, Cara." He heard his own voice soften at her name, and his eyes flashed along the full length of her trim body, twice.

She stepped out of the car and headed to her apartment. Jonathan followed her in.

"I don't want to leave this open ended, Cara. Everything else is up in the air. The only one everyone seems to get along with is you, except maybe Thomas now that you've threatened him. I don't want to be at odds with you. Do we have a problem?" He wasn't going to let the conversation die before she assured him she wasn't going to cut him out of her plans.

"No, Jonathan, we don't have a problem." She gave him a playful smirk as she walked into her bedroom. Relieved at her show of confidence in him, and at her apparent ease with him, he waited a bit more comfortably while she packed her bag with a quick variety of comfortable clothes. As soon as she emerged with bag in hand, they left for Jonathan's apartment.

The drive was uneventful and quiet, Jonathan wrapped in thought at the upcoming need to track down Christian. The adrenaline that had driven them through the night so far was fading and Jonathan caught Cara nodding off. Shaking her head back to full vigor, she glanced over to see him silently chuckling.

"I forget sometimes just what a powerful foe sleep can be. Go ahead and take five if you want."

Cara smiled a bit wryly and retorted, "And let you carry me into your apartment again? We've given that doorman enough fuel."

After parking the car in his usual stall in the parking garage, Jonathan pulled Cara's bag from the back seat while she scanned for trouble signs. The doorman smiled when he recognized Cara, winked at Jonathan, and probably harbored secret thoughts that he would savor all night.

At the apartment door, Cara took her bag from Jonathan while he unlocked the door, then led her into his bare apartment. She sat on the couch while Jonathan went to retrieve the book.

Holding the volume securely in both hands, he stepped into the living room and came within an arm's length of his guest. She looked at the blood red cover and Jonathan knew exactly what she was wondering: *is that human skin?*

"What does Thomas have against witches?" Cara asked.

"It's not my story to tell," Jonathan said quietly, knowing that particular answer was not going to satisfy her.

"Thomas can be informed of my every thought, but he's allowed all the secrets he wants? That's fair. And open. And honest." Cara glared at him.

Jonathan gritted his teeth. "We'll never get through this if we don't find some common ground. Maybe you can relax while you wait for Mason to call. I have some calls of my own to make." Jonathan retreated to his bedroom and left Cara alone once again.

The hours caught up to Cara once more. She could not continue at this pace of staying awake during the day trying to find Christian and at night fighting off his minions. And her attraction to Jonathan was getting in the way. She found herself watching him move, listening to him talk. Eventually, she couldn't help but drift off to sleep.

The instant his lips made contact with her skin, her eyes popped open and she saw him above her in his living room. He pulled back slightly and froze, as though he were trying but unable to read her.

Cara felt like someone had given her an electric shock. Lust, more base than she knew could exist within her, seared through her chest, her head, and her midsection. Not only her own but Jonathan's. His touch conveyed how much he wanted her. She tried to keep it all in check but lost the battle when Jonathan's fingers brushed her lips tenderly. Heat snaked through her and her heart began to pound. She caught an image of her naked body and his tongue. Keeping her own arousal in check was one thing; controlling both was another.

Her pulse racing, Cara put her hand on the back of his neck and pulled his head down to her. Their mouths met, already open. Tongues immediately stroked. He caught her around her waist and slowly, firmly, brought her up to meet him. His chest constricted as her nipples tightened through intervening material. She felt her passion lower her defenses, just as his had done to hers. With a growl he swung her up and carried her to his bed.

Mouths never parting, they crashed together onto the bed, and he fitted himself between her thighs, grinding his arousal against her. She moaned and wrapped one leg around his, running her bare foot up and down his thigh, across his tightened butt, pressing and smoothing as instinct taught her. Jonathan released her lips and relieved her of her blouse with one hand, bringing his head down to lick the valley between her breasts. His sensitive hands cupped them, and as he turned his attention to her nipples Cara's fingers gripped his back. Feeling his tongue through her bra was erotic, but she wanted skin to skin. He read her mind and, without bothering with the clasp, ripped the bra open and nipped her with his teeth. She cried out and felt her cry ignite his blood. He tore off his own shirt and returned to her mouth, rubbing his bare chest to hers.

He continued the rhythm with their lower bodies. Her fingers went to his belt, but he stopped her and removed hers with only slightly more regard than he had shown her bra. When she was naked he quickly stood and took off the rest of his own clothes in savage but effective pulls, as if his very life depended on the speed with which he disrobed. Cara had only just realized he was gone when he returned to nestle himself between her legs. She shivered when she felt him completely. His hand touched her wetness, and he nibbled and kissed a path down her body as she lay helpless, the waves of his passion washing over her with a power she had never felt in her entire life. Reaching his destination, he hooked her legs over his shoulders and buried his head to devour her.

Cara's hands fisted tightly in the sheets as his tongue streaked inside of her. Her hips rose up off the bed when he found her most sensitive part and sucked ruthlessly. The orgasm slammed into her unexpectedly, and Jonathan slid up her body but still didn't enter her; instead he rocked his penis against her as waves of pleasure continued to move within her and moisture seeped out of her. At last she was able to open her eyes and focus on him. He stopped his movements completely. Throwing his head back and his chest forward, he savored her heat and the feel of her well-toned legs wrapped around his waist. She placed her hands against his chest murmuring, "I want you in me, now." Sliding her hands down his chest and across his stomach, she relaxed the grip her legs had on him, opening wider and at the same time sliding her hands around his waist to pull him inward.

He positioned himself quickly, slid his heat in slowly, only to remove himself before he was completely enveloped. Cara opened her mouth to protest, anticipation already building. Before she could form words, he entered her again, pushed slightly deeper and longer, then once more retreated. She was stretched almost to the point of pain. He continued the torture until one thrust buried him to the hilt. Her hips lifted to receive him, if not to take him.

Then she felt it change. He had smelled the blood. Only a few drops but to his heightened senses it might as well have been oceans.

"No." His voice was hoarse. His arms began to tremble as he supported himself over her. Cara opened her eyes and saw the last thing she expected— anger! His pupils dilated and his teeth became fangs. "You—should—have—told—me." Each word was punctuated by a thrust, and even though the mood had changed she could feel herself responding. He seemed to battle with himself and lose.

Jonathan threw his head back and roared. He collapsed onto one elbow and grabbed her leg behind the knee, pushing it over his shoulder so he could drive into her hard and fast. He pounded into her and as her second release poured over him physically and mentally, he slammed into her body one last time as he came.

He lay fully on her. She was still throbbing. He slid out of her body and left the bed. He looked over her, anger still on his face. "Clean yourself up," he snarled at her before he slammed into the bathroom.

Cara lay numbly for a moment and listened to several pieces of glass break behind the closed door. Fury ignited in her as well. She hadn't realized her virginity was such an issue. She snatched up her clothes, leaving her useless bra, and went into the guest bathroom. She dressed and left before Jonathan could emerge from his self-imposed cage.

CHAPTER 19

The first thing Cara did was steal Jonathan's car. She called Mason on her cell phone and had him meet her at her apartment. He didn't ask any questions when Cara told him they were no longer going to be working with Jonathan and Thomas.

Cara took the files that Mason had picked up from the station and got into her car, nodded thanks to Mason, and headed back to Beth's. By this time, all desire for sleep had totally fled her body, and a new surge of adrenaline was dominating her system. Vaguely, she was aware that it would all catch up with her, but she hoped by then to be safely within the protective walls of her friend's home. When she arrived at Beth's, the morning light was beginning to break. Warned by Sheena that she had company, Beth met her at the door. When Cara headed straight for the phone, Beth was smart enough to get out of the way. Cara dialed Thomas' number and waited.

"Watterson," answered the voice on the other end.

"Just thought I'd give you some good news." Cara was in full control now, and no one in their right mind would try to make it otherwise.

"You found Christian?" Thomas asked.

"No. But you no longer need to check in with Beth. The only person you need to check in with is Jonathan. You don't need to meet here tonight either. We will not be continuing our tenuous partnership any longer. I'm sure you'll be thrilled." With that she hung up the receiver.

"Well, that was to the point!" Beth said sardonically when Cara hung up. "Are you going to fill me in?" Cara gave her as much information as she could without going into unnecessary detail.

"Wow." Beth sat there with her head in her hands. "You really know how to shatter a girl's fantasy about the first time."

Cara had never before been intimate with anyone because she wasn't sure she could handle someone in close proximity. Beth—well it was hard to meet someone when you hadn't left your house in six years.

"Let's get to the matter at hand. We aren't going to be getting that book. We need to find other ways to at least protect ourselves." Cara dismissed the problem with Jonathan from her mind but it pissed her off how hard she was working at burying the hurt.

"I'll make a list of things that actually deter vampires. I'll see if I can find any spells that might help. Are you staying here?" Beth asked.

"Yes, I stopped and got a map and some flags. I want to go through the files Mason gave me to see if I can pinpoint an area where Christian might be." Beth nodded and left for her library.

Cara spread out her map. She would have to go through the files first and see what matched the crimes she was looking for. Gruesomely boring work, but someone had to do it.

"She said what?" Jonathan asked in disbelief from the end of the phone line.

"She said we were no longer in a tenuous partnership," Thomas repeated.

"Does she think she can just ask Christian to leave her alone and he will?" Thomas could hear him pacing.

"No, she thinks she can hunt him down and destroy him. Cara doesn't strike me as the ask nicely type. Of course, you've never seen her shoot anyone. You should have seen her take out that guy at Beth's, she didn't flinch." Thomas stopped and when there was no sound on the other end he said, "Jonathan?"

"I'm here. I thought you didn't like her..."

"I never said I didn't like her. I was wary at first, but she's okay. It's her side kick that I don't care for," Thomas retorted.

"So it's okay with you if we continue on our own?"

Jonathan rarely asked for opinions or advice, and Thomas didn't let it pass by. "You're asking *me*? What's going on?"

"We haven't involved anyone in our business for a long time. Do we leave them to their own devices and hope we can stop Christian before they cross his path again, or do we mend fences and work together, if that's possible?"

"I don't know, Jonathan," Thomas replied sincerely. "When she first called I was only too glad to make the break, but as much as I hate to say it, I have this feeling that splitting up could be a bad thing." Sometimes the only thing he had to go on was instinct and his was telling him to band together.

"We go to Beth's tonight," Jonathan stated loudly, suddenly coming to a decision. "We'll take the book as a peace offering. We'll have to make them see it our way. I think you're right. We are going to need their help."

"Why do we need a peace offering? Cara is the one who called it off!" Now Thomas was truly puzzled.

"Don't ask!" and with that Jonathan disconnected. Thomas wondered what in the world his friend had done. Left with nothing he wanted to contemplate, he returned to his work.

Cara and Beth took a nap in the afternoon to prepare for the evening ahead. With Sheena and the spells watching over them, Cara felt safe and slept. They awoke mid-afternoon only to continue their search for information. Mason arrived an hour before sundown and gave Cara a large stack of files.

"I had Barry go back further and narrow the search to a few specifics."

"I hope you didn't give him too many," Cara said, setting the files aside for now.

"Not enough to have me talking to the department psychiatrist. Do you want to go first or shall I?" Cara let him review his findings.

"The station is half crazy, they set up lines for information and last night we had several reports of random attacks. Like small massacres. It's a mess. And we have some very skilled citizens giving us a hand. Three reports came in of people being attacked and then rescued by what they thought was a SWAT team but it wasn't us. I also noticed that Vinton was hanging around the guys on the task force we set up since the attack. He didn't seem to be helping, but he was definitely all eyes. Barry said he'd been hanging around his office, too. No specific questions, just idle chitchat."

"What do you think he wants?" Cara asked.

"No idea, but I'll be keeping an eye on him."

"How many eyes do you have, Mason?" Cara joked.

"At least one more to go over the maps with," he smiled back.

As they looked over the maps to see if they could distinguish any patterns, Beth took a break to fix dinner.

CHAPTER 20

ow do you cook like that every night and not weigh four hundred pounds?" Mason asked Beth as they cleared away the dishes.

"I don't cook like that every night, and I certainly don't eat like that every night, but when I have company I like to pull out all the stops." Dinner was Beth's hour to keep her hands busy and let the information sink in and connect. Beth laughed on her way to the kitchen—ignoring the way they both watched her; trying to pretend that it was a normal evening at home while waiting for her to tell them they were about to be attacked by a pack of hell-raising vampires.

Beth had compiled a list of ways to ward off or repel them. After dinner they sat and went over it. Garlic, unfortunately, was not on the list. Of all the things on the list, *that* would have been the easiest to find.

"First on my list is a spell that will protect you from becoming a vamp or slave; you will actually have to give your permission to fall under that influence."

"But could they still kill us?" Mason interrupted.

"Yes, but you won't come back at the bidding of your master," Beth said with a meaningful look.

"That has its merits," Mason agreed.

"Silver bullets, swords, or daggers, actually anything made from pure silver will slow them down. It will not kill them, but they won't heal from those wounds as fast. There's a potion of sorts that can harm them also, but it's a kind of hair-of-the-dog-that-bit-you sort of thing. You have to have the blood of the vamp that made them. We're not likely to get that. Would be handy though, it acts like acid on their skin."

"They can't be invincible, can they?" Mason asked without much hope in his voice. "There has to be some way to kill them without being close enough to remove their hearts, not to mention getting them to sit still long enough for you to do it. The only reason it worked the other night was because of your spell, Beth. Otherwise we'd be toast. And where the hell am I supposed to find silver bullets?" he ended in exasperation.

"I know a person that can get those for you, but they are expensive," Beth said, smiling.

"I'll pay," Mason assured her.

"All right, first a lesson on the history of vampires. You both need to have a better understanding of what we're dealing with," Beth began. Almost as quickly as she did, she paused and tilted her head. Mason and Cara sat up straight, both reaching for their guns.

"Don't worry, you two. It's not the company you might think it is. If I'm not mistaken, it's Thomas and Jonathan. They mean no harm." She added the last because neither Mason nor Cara had removed their hands from their weapons. She looked squarely at Cara. "I think we should hear them out."

"I think we should try out some of your repellents," Mason offered.

"They wouldn't have any effect on Thomas." Beth gave Mason a stern *behave yourself* look.

"I think the silver bullets would have the desired effect," Mason grinned. She appreciated that he knew he was losing and chose to go down gracefully.

"I have a feeling it might not affect him the way you think," Beth said slyly.

"What? How many freakin' things am I supposed to deal with at once?" Mason's outraged cry served to break the tension as Cara and Beth had to smother a laugh. "I don't even like the other world, and here I am right in the damn middle of it." He grumbled all the way to the door.

When Beth nodded, he opened it and met Thomas' raised hand that was about to knock.

"And you say they're not spooky," Thomas said to Jonathan, his tone light. "May we come in?"

Beth followed Cara's eyes toward Jonathan and nodded her answer. Jonathan entered, carrying a black leather briefcase at his side; high tech and high security by the looks of it. Knobs and dials that Beth was hard pressed to identify.

"Thomas and I both believe we would all be better served if we worked together," Jonathan said as soon as he had taken a seat across from Cara. Mason resumed his seat on the couch, putting his arm around the back behind Cara and leaning a little closer to her, as though claiming her in front of Jonathan. He smiled and looked innocently at the vampire across the room. Jonathan stiffened.

"Enough!" Cara said sharply, openly looking back and forth between the two of them. "You two are spilling out so much testosterone, Beth and I are going to grow chest hair. I don't belong to you, Mason." He glared and Jonathan relaxed. "And I definitely don't belong to you either."

"At least I didn't get definitely," Mason smirked. When Cara muttered an, "Oh, Lord help me," and dropped her head into her hands, Mason relented. "I was only kidding." She lifted her head and gave him a weak smile. Mason pulled his arm back around and placed his hand safely in his lap.

"We come with a peace offering." Without further ceremony he fiddled with the briefcase for a moment and it sprang open.

Beth gasped at what she saw inside. Everyone looked at her.

"That book doesn't just have protection spells, it contains true power!" She wasn't in any hurry to touch it. "I was just about to explain a little about the history of vampires. I thought it might help to know more about what we're dealing with. I'm sure you're well versed, Jonathan, but you'll have to bear with us."

Everyone settled around the chair Beth occupied like children getting ready for a bedtime story. She looked around, no "happily ever afters" here.

"In the beginning, vampires were much different than what we are dealing with today. Vampires started out as guardians. Mortals couldn't always fight their enemies, so Vampires did it for us." She ignored the raised eyebrows, including Jonathan's; perhaps he didn't know as much as she thought he did. "Mortals gave up their blood freely to their defenders and friends, a gift if you will; there is no requirement to kill to attain blood to enhance a vampire's skills and power.

"Unfortunately, like any species, there were those who felt they didn't need to serve. They felt they were the ones who should be served. When rebellion began, the guardians, vampires that believed in protecting, called up every force and power they had access to and bound all vampires to a code of conduct. For example, they could not kill one another for fear of a punishment unimaginable. They made it harder for vampires to expand to a large number, after all, their original goal was to protect us; if the protectors outnumbered the protected, they would soon make mortals extinct simply from supplying food.

"I've never found a mention as to what the punishment was, but I did find an instance of two vampires in a pack going to battle: at the end one was dead. Never again did I find mention of one vampire killing another. And that entry was so old that even now just the threat is enough of a deterrent." She glanced at Jonathan.

"The original guardians found a way to transcend the human form. They still watch to keep the rest in line, but they are bound by the same laws. They are much like the governors that witches have. The vampires we are dealing with today are a sort of mutated strain. If it makes you feel any better, Mason, I doubt they are as powerful as they once were. We would have far greater problems on our hands if they had the power they once did." As she stopped speaking, she noticed the rest of the small group was looking at Jonathan, as if seeing him for the first time. This information changed him from a renegade do-gooder to a descendant of the original strain of vampires, a sort of prince among thieves. Jonathan himself had a dazed expression on his face.

"How do you know all of this?" Jonathan asked. "I've looked for centuries and never came up with any of that." He looked almost disbelieving, but then so did Mason. "How and when did we vampires earn the reputation we have? In the literature I've studied, there's no mention of vampires ever being anything but monsters." He looked at Cara when he said *monsters*.

"For the last six years I have done nothing but study the past, particularly legend and myth. I am also a witch." She looked at Thomas as if daring him to say something, but for once no snide remarks came from his corner. "I have access to books only seen by witches, records that mortals have no inkling of. I think we'll save the witches' history for another night though," she said with a grin. "You don't have access to that kind of information; furthermore, you do not even associate with your own kind, so I would assume that you are limited in your access to such records." She flicked a glance at Thomas, and he narrowed his eyes at her.

"It doesn't surprise me that you haven't found what you were looking for. The languages and symbols are not passed through mortal generations and are therefore not kept in their libraries and archives. As to why vampires are looked upon as monsters, the things I'm talking about happened a very, very long time ago. You've been around how many centuries? Three, give or take a few decades? After thousands of years of vampires being monsters, the original legend is erased as far as everyday mortals are concerned." Beth finished and sat back smugly. It wasn't often she had an audience, even a small one, to lecture to. She liked it.

"I'm not sure I like the way you keep saying *mortals*," Mason looked wary.

"Don't worry, Mason, there's not one of us in this room that is mere mortal, even you have abilities transcending normal humans." She slid another glance at Thomas, who stood to leave the room.

Mason had had enough of feeling like everyone in the room was one up on him. "I know what I am and I know what everybody else is, except Thomas. You want to explain it to me?"

"If I knew for sure, Mason, I would let you in on it. But frankly, I haven't a clue," Beth admitted.

"Great." Mason fell silent.

Thomas reentered the room but remained stubbornly silent. It was apparent he wasn't going to be spilling the beans anytime soon.

"Has it occurred to anyone else that it's extremely quiet tonight? I mean outside, not in," Cara ventured.

"I didn't want to jinx it," Mason said.

CHAPTER 21

Beth still looked at it as if she would rather forego touching the book. Sheena paced back and forth. Thomas returned to the room and stood beside Jonathan. Beth got up and walked over to them, rubbing sweaty palms on her jeans. Silently she held her hands out, and Jonathan gave it to her.

It hummed, beginning as a low guttural sound, then winding towards the high end of the sound chart—like a jet engine warming up on the runway. Beth could feel it steeling up her arms as her hands warmed. Scenes exploded in Beth's mind. Images flying too fast for her to focus on slowed until they moved in real time. A dark headed vampire rose from the ground, his hands and mouth dripping with bloody gore, the lifeless body ruined beyond anything that could be recognized as human. He opened his hand and there lay the chain with the mangled ring. Blood and entrails tangled with it as he slipped it over his head and another vampire entered.

"Christian! The sun is coming, we must leave. Did you find it?"

"Yes, and with it the earth is mine," Christian whispered.

Beth watched them leave but was unable to force herself from the vision. She could feel the book warming even more in her hands. Over the body of the slain man light shimmered. A man's shape formed but it was hazy.

He spoke directly to her. "Child. You must put an end to Christian. He must never get the elder charm back, or the book. On the anniversary of the ascension he will be able to turn as many vampires as he wishes and those turned will be empowered to do the same. The power from the book will last a single year, and by the end of that time humanity will be enslaved."

"But… "

"No time for questions. You must let go." The voice grew harsh. "Release the book! Now!"

Beth couldn't speak, couldn't move. Light exploded behind her eyes, illuminating the aura that surrounded each of the others in the room. She screamed, as her body was suddenly enflamed and burning. Beth dropped the book and crumpled.

Thomas reached for her, even as she was falling, she yanked herself out of his reach, sheer terror on her face.

"Not you! Don't touch me. He's—he's—a Vishka! I should have seen it. I should have known. I—I—I . . ." her voice trailed off and she didn't finish, couldn't finish. She lay on the floor, trembling and wild-eyed as she stared at Thomas. Cara knelt beside her and gently looked at her hands. The flesh had bubbled.

"Mason, under the sink there's a first aid kit, bring it to me." With a look guaranteeing pain to someone, Mason did as Cara requested.

"What did you do to her?" Mason spat out as he brought a huge box into the living room. "If this is your idea of a peace offering, you've been out of the human race longer than I thought." Beth's sobs had subsided under Cara's protective arms, and she sat with her head against the chair, breathing deeply. As Cara cleaned the burns, tears slid down her cheeks. "Hey, Beth?" Mason tried to get her attention. "Do you normally perform minor surgery? That box looks like it came right out of an operating room." His tone was a bit forced as he tried to get her mind off the pain in her hands.

"I just make sure I have what I need for any emergency," she said in a voice that sounded rusty. The box Mason had brought was full of everything one needed to tend a wounded army, well, at least a small patrol.

Jonathan and Thomas stood in the background, both looking as if they should leave. Mason and Cara settled Beth on the couch after Cara had given her something for the pain, and everyone stood, silently and awkwardly. After the medication kicked in, she sat up slowly and surveyed them all.

"He didn't do it on purpose." Beth relayed all she had seen and it was the power the Ancients had used that caused the problem.

"How are your hands?" Jonathan asked.

Beth was drained and she sank on the couch. "They'll heal. Until then I have some great pain medication," she grinned.

"I'm sorry. I didn't know. I thought all I had to do was hand it over." Jonathan looked as though he wished there was something more he could do.

Before Beth could reply, Thomas said, "It's not your fault." He said it harmlessly enough, no bite in his tone, but Beth jumped at him just the same. She was in his face before anyone realized her intention.

"You don't speak in my house, scavenger! You have no place here except quietly at Jonathan's side. The only reason I haven't expelled you is because of him. He must have a good reason for dragging you around." Beth felt her violet eyes glowing with intensity and Thomas took a step back. Mason looked shocked, but he made no move to end her standoff. Cara stared very deliberately at Thomas, like she was silently reminding him of her earlier threat. Jonathan stood at Thomas' side, but all things considered, he looked outnumbered.

"I think we'd better go—" Thomas began, but Beth cut him off again.

"*Do not speak!*" she yelled, her voice amplified and distorted as if she were speaking in many voices. Everyone except Cara physically jumped. The halo that Thomas had seen that first night formed around her head, her bandaged palms spread outward, and she advanced on Thomas. He went for the door but it didn't open. Jonathan tried to help him in vain as Beth's voice filled the air in a low chant. "Witches tried and always true, give this evil his rightful due. Return this demon to his place. Take away his stolen face!"

The halo stretched and surrounded her whole body. When

Jonathan couldn't budge the door, he turned and looked at Cara, as though what he was about to do would separate them forever. He started toward Beth, but Mason shot him in the shoulder. He went down but popped right back up. Thomas jumped toward Mason, who was probably not used to seeing his victims bounce back up like Jonathan just had and Thomas caught him with a vicious left hook that sent him sprawling on the couch. Cara flew across the room and planted herself firmly between Beth and Jonathan.

"This is where secrets get you. Everybody plays by the rules but you two. If you want her, you'll have to come through me and I won't go down easy." She pulled a dagger from behind her back. The silver blade gleamed and Jonathan raised his eyes to hers. The dead man was back.

"What makes you think I want it easy?" He smiled and his teeth elongated to fangs.

All around them Beth's power grew; she was almost floating now. Her voice still rang out as she chanted, "Governors and judges on high, do not this plea deny!"

Jonathan lunged and had Cara on pure speed, but when her hand flew up he encountered a wall and the slice of her blade. Blood dripped down his arm and for a split second he looked at her, disbelieving.

"Getting stronger, huh?"

Cara was gathering every emotion and surrounded herself with it.

"It didn't keep me out earlier did it, Cara?"

She hesitated for a second, but when he tried to move forward he hit her shimmering anger.

"Sex with a monster, everyone should try it once."

Jonathan surged forward screaming in rage as he tore through her wall. She brought her blade up and caught him under the ribs. In return, he shoved her to the ground and pinned her there.

"Beth! Beth!" Jonathan yelled. She caught him in her line of vision and stopped her chant, but the light around her didn't dim. "Stop now or she's gone. We'll explain everything, but you have to stop."

Beth wasn't about to move. Mason and Thomas stopped fighting, although it looked as though Mason had stopped it by putting Thomas' head through the wall. Jonathan saw Beth's hesitation and looked down at Cara, whose eyes widened. She started to struggle. He held her down easily, but with each movement the dagger she had stuck in his side dug a little deeper.

The room quieted at once and the light disappeared. Jonathan jumped up and moved as far from Cara as he could. He jerked the dagger from his side and threw it at her feet. She picked it up, cleaned it off on the towel she had used for Beth, and re-sheathed it behind her back.

Thomas stood up and staggered back to Jonathan. He seemed a little surprised to find Jonathan bleeding.

"Explain," Beth demanded.

Thomas opened his mouth, but her head snapped in his direction and her eyes flashed. He shut it just as quickly.

"Why did you call him a Vishka?" Jonathan asked.

"His kind feed on the weak willed. Stealing mortal bodies and casting their souls to the unknown. Most have powerful souls that don't want to die, so they seek bodies they can use. Since two souls cannot inhabit the same body, the weaker one is cast out." She looked at Thomas feeling disgust flowing out of herself. "Some nerve you had coming in here preaching to me about evil witches, you parasite."

"Why didn't you see it right away?"

"I don't read auras. I sense things, good and bad. I never sensed anything wrong coming from him. I assume it was because he meant no harm at that particular time. It wasn't until I held the book that I could see it. It illuminated the auras of everyone in this room. His was nothing. The only thing that surrounded him was an outline of red. That's death. A soul died in that body, but it wasn't his." She spat out that last word, unable to bring herself to use his name.

"I can explain. It's not what you think." Jonathan looked at Thomas as if asking for permission to continue. Thomas nodded.

CHAPTER 22

"Thomas is cursed. One hundred and twenty years ago, Thomas' father promised a witch named Jeferin a certain gift of power in exchange for healing his wife. He claimed to have a witch's amulet, into which that witch had spun all of her power. Thomas knows his father believed the amulet would bring power to the person who wore it and knew how to use it, but as he had no witching abilities himself he couldn't access that power. As agreed, after Jeferin healed his wife, he gave Jeferin the amulet, but when she put it on, she discovered that either it had no power or she did not possess the knowledge to bring it forth. In her anger she killed his father and mother, but that did not satisfy her. She cast Thomas' soul from his body.

"Jeferin was apparently not the brightest witch. We think she meant his soul to drift aimlessly, or, since you brought it up, send him into the unknown. However, Thomas can take over when a soul leaves a body. He never forces anyone out. Usually it's a person that has lost the will to live. He can't repair damage to a body so the body must be salvageable."

"You must spend a lot of time in hospitals."

Jonathan appreciated that Mason wasn't one to let a good jab pass by. Thomas' face darkened, but he said nothing. "No he doesn't," Jonathan responded, adding a tone of warning to his voice. "He has spent a lot of time wandering aimlessly. He doesn't hang over people's deathbeds. And you wonder why he didn't want anyone to know. It's hardly a lifestyle that he brags about to everyone he meets." Jonathan directed the last bit to Cara who seemed like she was trying to digest this new information.

"You idiot," Beth said mockingly from the couch as she started to laugh. "Jeferin isn't a real witch. She wanted to be one, but she screwed up everything she touched. I have the whole story somewhere. To be fair, she apparently had a small measure of talent, but she thought she could skip steps here and there and still end up with the same results." Beth sank into the couch, and Jonathan noted that her energy level was taking a dive. Thomas started to speak, then stopped, looking at Beth. She nodded.

"She did heal my mother. And look what she did to me. How do you know that story off the top of your head?"

"We use Jeferin's story as a kind of Aesop's fable to show us what would happen if we didn't give full credit to each of our actions." Beth's next words came out softer. "Thomas, chances are that your mother would have died soon anyway. Jeferin had healed people many times, but the healing was always temporary. Her victim's life was prolonged, but the person soon died of the very illness that she supposedly cured them of." She paused and Jonathan saw a sharpness come over her face. "And I am supposed to believe you? We all are supposed to take your word for everything, but we don't get the same consideration? If you want to go on hating me, fine, but we need to settle this now. We almost killed each other tonight."

Thomas seemed lost in thought for a moment; then he looked up at everyone and sighed. "Okay, clean slate. Everyone agreed?"

They looked at each other and nodded. Jonathan couldn't help but wonder if beating the crap out of each other was group therapy.

"To close this chapter for good, I have a question," said Thomas. "What happened to Jeferin?"

Beth looked lost in thought for a moment before she spoke. "Even though Jeferin wasn't a true witch, she dabbled in our business. She wanted to be one so badly that they eventually brought her before the governors. Her punishment was to suffer each of the illnesses she had supposedly cured. At the end of her time, she was put to death.

We're big on getting exactly what you deserve. We also like long punishments." Her eyes shifted to Cara's for a second before looking back at Thomas.

Jonathan caught the look and wondered what it meant. *Now who was keeping secrets?*

CHAPTER 23

The house was quiet while Jonathan paced in front of the plywood-covered windows. It wouldn't be so bad if he could see into the night. Luckily Beth had the panes being replaced in the morning. An hour ago they had decided it would be best if everyone retired for the evening. Beth took the book to read it, suffering no ill effect this time. Christian was taking extreme measures to retrieve the elder ring and small skirmishes were breaking out all over. Beth had given warning to all of the Otherkin that wouldn't be able to defend themselves. She'd also enlisted Otherkin that would find nothing but pleasure in bloody fights. They agreed it was Jonathan who should take watch. This, after all, was his time.

The night was passing without any sign of Christian or his minions and Jonathan was going with the notion that this was the quiet before the storm. He had tried to engage Cara in a quiet conversation but to no avail. *Must be nice to simply dismiss emotions into an abyss.*

Beth had three bedrooms, which was good because he couldn't honestly see Mason and Thomas sharing one. The truce was still precarious, but he no longer felt that they were their own worst enemies. They may still kill each other, but at least they would wait until Christian was taken care of. Jonathan heard a noise in the kitchen and went to investigate. He found Cara getting a glass of water.

"Everything okay?" he asked quietly.

"I'm up in the middle of the night getting my best friend pain medication because her hands are charred, but yeah, sure, everything is fine." Cara turned and took the pills out of the cabinet.

"I didn't plan it. I had no idea the effect it would have on her." Jonathan had spent a good amount of his pacing berating himself for

105

Beth's pain. He should have known that nothing was ever as simple as it should be.

"Funny you should put it that way. Were you thinking the same thing this morning?" Cara turned to walk out of the room when Jonathan snagged her arm.

"I wanted to talk to you earlier about that," Patience had never been his strong suit.

"I won't stand out here with you and chat while Beth is in pain." Cara jerked her arm out of his grasp and went back into the bedroom.

He tried to shrug off the remark. Deep down did she really feel he was some aberration, some… thing? Jonathan thought she was gone for the night and was surprised when a few minutes later she walked into the living room and sat on the couch.

"Talk," Cara said.

"First, I want to straighten out you and me," Jonathan began. He didn't know how she would like it if he sat beside her, so he took the seat across from her and spoke quietly.

"There is no you and me," Cara responded. "There is you unattached and there is me unattached, but there is no you and me together." Her voice remained calm but firm.

"I don't hop into bed with every woman I meet. When I do it's with careful consideration. There is something between us, and you felt it, too. You had to feel something," Jonathan almost wanted to shake her. Really he just wanted his hands on her body again, but his chances were slim to none. "I'm sorry if I scared you. I just wasn't prepared for what happened."

"You didn't scare me. You pissed me off. I wasn't any more prepared than you." Cara wasn't giving.

"Look, sex is a precarious thing for me. Senses are heightened, and it makes me crave blood. Not just blood but all the passion flowing through it. Can you imagine having both desires flowing through you at once? Can you imagine what it was like to be inside you, to hunger for you in a different way and then smell blood, even a drop? I didn't want to hurt you and feared I was going to. I don't like my control shaken like that." Jonathan had never explained any of that to anyone. He sensed that the only way he would ever get her at his side was to be honest.

"I know what you felt. That's what made it so hard for me to back away. My feelings I could control; both together were impossible." Cara relaxed against the back of the couch.

"Does that mean I'm forgiven?" Jonathan sounded wary.

"Yes." It was almost inaudible, as if she still wasn't sure.

Jonathan moved to sit beside her. He took her face in both hands and turned her to look at him. It was on the tip of his tongue to ask her how she really saw him but he felt stripped bare as it was. "You don't sound so sure."

"Yes, Jonathan, you're forgiven." Cara's voice was firm and very understandable.

He pulled her forward and kissed her.

She returned it until she felt the stirrings of his need, then she pushed him away gently. "I don't know where this can go, Jonathan. If not for this situation we never would have met. I don't know if I want to continue seeing you after it's over. We've only known each other for four days and we've already tried to kill each other. You were ready to rip out my throat and I was prepared to carve out your heart. I don't think something like that bodes well for a future."

"No offense, Cara, but I could have taken you or Beth at any time. You've seen how fast I can move, and that's without concentrating. You maybe could have taken me as well, but that's a huge maybe." He laughed as she punched him in the arm in indignation, but sobered as he continued. "You aren't going to like this but I'm going to tell you anyway. You are mine." He pulled her closer, but the grin had left her face. "You won't run from me again, because next time I'll come after you. You can try not to see me when this is over, but I won't back off until we see whatever this is to the end."

"And what happens if the end leaves us on opposite sides?" Cara removed herself from his touch.

CHAPTER 24

When the phone rings at 4:00 A.M. it's usually bad news. Thomas didn't have to rouse anyone, they were all standing there waiting when he hung up the phone, feeling extremely confused.

"The police just picked up Valerie." He focused on Jonathan. "Our men can't interfere with the police. Tony was not happy about sitting back and watching."

"Who's Valerie?" Mason asked, pulling his shirt over his head.

"My secretary." Jonathan's face shut down.

"That's not the confusing part. Before they took her away, Tony managed to get the name of the officer arresting her. Danny Brooks."

"What!" Mason stopped in the middle of putting his shoulder holster on.

"According to Tony, the officer identified himself as Danny Brooks. He also got his badge number." Thomas recited it and Cara verified that it was Danny's.

"Mason, call the station and find out what's going on with Valerie. What's her last name, Jonathan?" Jonathan gave Mason her last name and Mason picked up the phone. "Thomas, call Tony back and ask for a description. Anyone can rent a cop's uniform and get a badge number."

Thomas grabbed his cell phone and called Tony back. Beth started making coffee for everyone and took a diet Coke for herself; the bandages made the process awkward and she struggled to open the can. From the corner of his eye Thomas saw Beth fighting with the can; he reached over, took it from her, opened it, and handed it back. It was a simple thing, but Beth stared at the can in wonderment. Thomas clicked off and got everyone's attention.

"Light brown hair, five-ten, one hundred eighty-five pounds, and an attitude the size of Texas." Thomas closed his notebook and poured a cup of coffee.

"Danny was six-two, two hundred fifteen pounds, with hair so blond it was almost white. Unless Tony's eyes are failing him there is no question that this was not Danny."

Mason interrupted, "There is no record of a Valerie Gordon being picked up for any reason. No one has any idea what I'm talking about. But there is a squad car missing from motor pool."

"How do you steal a police car?" Thomas asked.

"Be a cop," Cara said soberly.

"Maybe there's been a mix-up somewhere. If she really did go with the police, she would at least get a phone call. I'll see what numbers she has at the office and look up her emergency contact." Jonathan began collecting his phone and briefcase, then stopped and turned to Beth.

"I only have a few hours until sunrise, but I'm going to try to get back here, safety in numbers and all that. Can I borrow a bed for the day?" Jonathan made the request of Beth, but he was watching Cara.

"If things keep going like this I'm going to have to add on. I don't do laundry."

Mason decided to go to headquarters and see if he could find out any more information.

When everyone left, Cara and Beth stared across the table at each other. "Donuts," they said at the same time. Beth pulled a box out from her pantry, and they sat in the kitchen and ate until fatigue began to set in again. Deciding to sleep while they still could, they went back to bed.

CHAPTER 25

Jonathan drove carefully to his office, praying that there was a simple explanation for Valerie's disappearance, not allowing himself to give credit to any other scenarios. If Christian had her, he'd be hearing about it soon enough.

"You're awfully quiet this morning, Thomas," Jonathan said.

"Do you believe Beth? I was comparing Jeferin with Beth. I only met Jeferin once, well, twice if you count when she showed up to rip me from my body. I didn't like her. I tried to talk my father out of bargaining with her. His desire to have my mother healed made him blind to Jeferin's deceit. I don't get any bad vibes from Beth," Thomas admitted reluctantly as he pushed himself down in the seat in a sulk.

"I agree. I don't see Cara being involved with anyone not on the up and up." Jonathan hoped Thomas would get past his problem with Beth.

"You haven't known Cara for that long," Thomas pointed out.

"I've been inside her . . ." the words brought up an image of Cara underneath him and he stumbled on his words, "her mind."

Thomas sat up straight in his seat and looked at Jonathan. "Is there something going on I should know about?"

"There is definitely nothing you should know," Jonathan said firmly.

Thomas studied Jonathan's profile and started to chuckle. "You slept with her. She's got your tongue tied." Jonathan studiously ignored Thomas.

They arrived at the office building and Jonathan looked up at the sky knowing he would be stuck at the office for the day. They were silent as the elevator made its way smoothly to the top floor. The doors opened with a swish, and the stench assaulted them. Thomas stumbled and gagged. Jonathan walked ahead, then stopped as if he had run into a wall. Thomas moved up to stand next to Jonathan, and Valerie's desk came into view.

The blood left Thomas' face. Jonathan had nearly the opposite reaction, as the anger began to drive blood to his head, trying to force a change that he worked hard to control. Once again, his will drove back his body's need to rampage.

Valerie lay naked on her desk, the tile floor around her littered with the paraphernalia of her work. Her face was twisted in terror; her eyes were wide and fixed. The skin of her neck was shredded and smeared, and angry red scratches marred her from breasts to knees, concentrating particularly on the inside of her battered thighs. What was left of her blood trailed down her arms, falling from her fingertips to the tiles below. Her legs were left open, one bent at an awkward angle.

Jonathan looked down at Valerie's abused body, his imagination filling in for him what had been done to her. Guilt weighed down what was left of his soul. He half stumbled around the desk, heading to his office when his eyes shifted back to the innocent girl sacrificed on the altar of Christian's anger. He stopped again and stared. Between her legs a gold letter opener impaled a piece of paper to the desk. He clamped his teeth together and retrieved the note.

J,

I do hope you had the pleasure of our little Valerie before we did. You'd be proud of her. She begged and pleaded like a good girl while we all had a go at her. To her credit, she had sufficient fear and blood to satisfy each of us and she held up admirably. I have a higher expectation of Cara. I hope you will tell her I'll be enjoying her soon. One of you has something that belongs to me and you've hidden it well. Return it or watch them die one by one. I wish you had more children.

C.

Blinding, white hot rage filled Jonathan, and he did not fight back. His skin paled. His teeth elongated, and a blankness covered his eyes.

"Jonathan, don't—"

"Don't what?" he hissed. "Don't get upset? Don't blame myself for her death? Don't rip that fucking bastard to pieces with my bare hands. Do you think this is the worst he can do?" He shoved the letter at Thomas. "This was almost kind for him. I've seen his atrocities. This is my fault. I was afraid I wasn't strong enough to kill him all those years ago, so I ran. I was a coward and Valerie paid for it." Jonathan turned and went to the phone in his office. He called Mason to discover what he was in for when the police came. Mason said he would come himself, but Jonathan declined, saying that he needed him to keep digging for Christian's location; however, he did ask Mason to call his fellow detectives. He would know how to best predispose them to not tie in the two businessmen with this murder in their office. While Jonathan waited for the police to arrive, he called Beth and gave her the news.

By the time the detectives showed up at the scene, Jonathan was in full control. Outwardly he was everything he was supposed to be. Inside he was thinking of what he was going to do to Christian and how much agony it was going to involve.

CHAPTER 26

Christian lay in his temporary home. He'd yet to change his bloody clothes. He often liked to keep his victim's blood close to him, he'd even been known to wallow in it, but that was such a waste. The secretary's death barely took the edge off his frustration and anger. He'd wanted it to be Cara but he wouldn't share her. He would keep her for himself to enjoy over and over. He got hard just thinking about the ways he would hurt her. She would give all of herself before it was over. He reached for the girl he kept for his pleasure, and grabbing her by her hair he shoved her to his crotch. She undid his pants with trembling fingers. Christian's mind blurred as she began to work him. He brought his hand to where the elder ring usually lay, the spot was empty and his anger exploded. He grabbed the girl and he didn't stop until her screams did.

CHAPTER 27

Cara and Beth sat at the kitchen table, absorbing the news of Valerie's death. "How is Jonathan taking this? How did he sound?" Cara asked.

"Hollow. I wouldn't want to be in his path right now." Beth fingered the condensation on her soda can. She couldn't drink anymore. There was a lump in her throat she couldn't get past.

Beth continued, "Christian wants to push him over the edge. He's got a plan. He would have killed Jonathan a long time ago if he could without repercussions. I think he's found a way around it. If he hadn't, he wouldn't be going after him this way."

Cara closed her eyes as Beth bolted up in her chair. "Someone's coming." The handyman whom she occasionally hired to do things around the house had already come earlier and replaced the windows. Beth liked him because he did good work and didn't ask too many questions. No, this was somebody else.

Cara shoved her chair away from the table and pulled out her gun. She grabbed the sword from beside the door and handed it to Beth.

"Wait. It's one person, not familiar, but no bad vibes." Beth still kept the sword and took a position beside the door opposite Cara. Sheena stood vigilant at a window, but did not bare her teeth or make a sound as she sniffed about, hoping to get a waft of the visitor's odor.

They heard the car pull up into the drive. Cara looked out the peep hole and told Beth she saw a van. The driver got out and rounded the back of the vehicle. He loaded three large cartons onto a dolly and headed towards the door.

"Well, it's your call, should we kill the messenger?" Cara asked Beth.

"Let's see what he's brought first." Beth raised the sword.

A knock sounded at the door.

"Yes?" Cara said.

"Delivery," a muffled voice replied.

"From who?"

"Uh, Schmidt."

Beth breathed in relief and whispered, "It's okay. As a matter of fact, it couldn't have come at a better time." Beth lowered the sword. Sheena lay down beneath the kitchen table, but kept her head up and eyes alert.

Cara tucked the gun behind her back and opened the door. She stepped back as Beth signed for the delivery. When the van drove away, Cara helped Beth carry the boxes inside. Actually, with Beth's size and her badly burned hands, Cara did most of the lifting, while Beth helped to guide the boxes through the doorway and into the house.

"What the hell are in these? They weigh a ton!" Cara was breathing heavily by the time they got all the boxes inside.

"Silver bullets." Beth collapsed on the sofa.

"All those! Are you kidding? Do you have any idea how many bullets are in each one of those boxes?" Cara looked stunned.

"There should be a crossbow with silver-tipped arrows, too. I don't know how to use a gun, but I'm hell with a crossbow. I didn't know what kind of guns you had, so Schmidt sent a couple of his own make, some kind of special weapon that fires faster. The more silver that gets into their bodies, the slower they're able to recover. As fast as vampires can move, these guns are supposed to help make sure the bullets get to where they're intended."

"Wow. You're right up there with Jonathan. You know people that can send you weapons overnight. When this is over, you and he should team up. You can slay' em, and he can have them cleaned up." Beth appreciated Cara's first smile of the day. "How do you get weapons delivered so easily? Most companies have safeguards for that sort of thing."

"Private delivery service." Beth looked to the front door. "Mason is on his way in."

Moments later, Mason knocked on the door.

"Somebody please tell me I'm having a nightmare. Never mind, I'm way too tired to be asleep." He dropped on the couch, laid his head back, and closed his eyes. "Jonathan will be tied up for hours. I told him that I would go myself, but he insisted I keep looking for Christian, who, by the way, I'm beginning to believe is invisible."

"It's only eleven," Cara said. "We have most of the day to find him."

"Swell, so we'll spend the whole day looking for him, and if, and I stress the *if*, we find him, we'll have had about four hours of sleep in a 48-hour period. Our exhaustion against their superhuman strength—I feel better already."

"Cranky, cranky!" Beth said. "I have just the thing to perk you up."

"You have a spell that will give me endless energy?" Mason looked suspicious.

"This surprise is going to lift your spirits naturally." Beth grinned. "Weapons."

"Weapons? Is that what's in these boxes?" Mason rose and began circling them, rubbing his hands together. "Can I open them?"

"Men and their toys. The crossbow is mine," Beth forewarned him.

"Can I at least try it?" Mason asked as he took a pocketknife out and began opening the boxes.

"I guess so, but you can't use the silver-tipped arrows. I've got regular ones you can practice with," Beth said.

"Whoa!" Mason pulled a wicked-looking handgun from the box. "What is this? It looks like a nine mil, but this extra mechanism, I've never seen." He held the weapon in front of him, checking the sight and the weight. "It's heavier, too." He looked into the box and pulled out a second weapon. "Ooh, two."

"That one is mine!" Cara jumped out of her chair and snatched it from his hand.

"Beth, she took my gun." Mason turned and gave Beth what could be considered a pout.

"There is something very wrong with this whole scene," Beth said as she laughed.

Mason shrugged and went into the box again. He pulled out the crossbow and after a close examination handed it to Beth. The second and third boxes held ammunition for all of the weapons. There must have been thousands of rounds.

For the next thirty minutes they continued to get used to their new weapons. There is much to be said for living in the middle of nowhere.

CHAPTER 28

Sleep. If only she could sleep. Christian knew where they were. Common sense told them they would be getting a visit after sundown. Cara looked at the clock again. She'd been able to sleep for two hours, but her mind was ready to go again. It was hard to sleep when you knew what an innocent woman's body was recently put through. Bagged, tagged, and, if the medical examiner thought it was important enough, Valerie was being weighed in pieces, picked over and picked through. Because the ME's office was habitually backlogged, and with terror finding its way into the streets, she could very well be lying in a cooler, covered by a thin sheet. *Was she watching from somewhere? Appalled by her treatment? Angry at being caught up in something she had no knowledge of?* Cara sighed, rolled over, and stared at the ceiling. It was easy for her to ask these questions unemotionally, an unconscious act. How was everyone else handling it?

Beth and Mason had spent the early afternoon teasing and laughing. Defense mechanism? Some shrinks would say so, or were the three of them so used to seeing horrible things that they were no longer affected as they should be? Cara and Mason spent most days wading through the nasty things humans did to each other. Vampires just did it faster.

The sound of Mason's cell phone broke into her maudlin thoughts. Cara got up, pulled on her jeans, and went to see if anyone else was dead.

Mason was just clicking off when Cara walked in. Beth was emerging from the library. Sleep didn't seem to be popular at the moment.

"That was the station. One of my snitches is requesting a meeting. He may have the info we're looking for." Mason took the new weapon and put it in his shoulder holster. The old one went into the back of his jeans. He loaded both with silver bullets. Cara did the same. "This is where we are meeting him." He scribbled an address down and handed it to Beth.

"Should I call Thomas and tell him?" Beth asked taking the slip of paper.

"As soon as we know what's going on, I'll call you. Then you can call Thomas and let him know." Mason watched as Cara loaded four extra clips with silver bullets. Sighing, he went to his duffle bag, pulled out four extra clips and did the same.

CHAPTER 29

Ernie wasn't a bad-looking guy. Five nine, about one hundred eighty-five pounds. Dark brown hair swept the top of his glasses; they masked brown eyes that hid intelligence. He was known to skirt the law. His past experience gave him a taste of the criminal life. So he made sure he stayed just on the right side of the line.

When they arrived at the bar, Ernie was playing pinball in the back. Cara leaned against the wall facing him, and Mason stood directly behind him. Ernie glanced up at Cara, started to smile, then whipped around to Mason.

"Shit, man! You shouldn't sneak up on people like that." Ernie glanced nervously between the two.

"So what's the word?" Mason knew Ernie's personal dealings weren't always on the up and up, but his information had never taken Mason down a wrong road so; he cut him some slack.

"Who's this?" Ernie eyed Cara suspiciously. Mason knew he didn't like dealing with other cops. The only reason he dealt with Mason was that he was the only one who had kept digging when Ernie got into trouble; the rest had just written him off.

"Detective Evens. She's okay, Ernie. You know I wouldn't bring someone else here unless I thought it was important." Mason said.

"Okay, but only because these guys really creeped me and *only* because I think they're out for you," Ernie said solemnly. He motioned them to the table.

"Spill," Mason said as he and Cara took a seat beside Ernie.

"I go to Jordan's all the time. Everybody knows I go there, and everybody knows you and I still have a beer now and then. Few days ago two guys come in, have a few drinks, and leave. Next night, same thing. Last night they strike up a conversation. Bullshit in the beginning—we're new in town, stuff like that—then they start talking about this cop that's looking for their boss. This cop is stupid, he'll never find him, blah, blah, blah. Then what do you think happens? One of them gets a phone call, takes down an address, and doesn't bother to hide it. They knew I would pass it on. Their mistake was thinking I was dumb enough to pretend I just came across the information. They want you, man, and I think they're playing for keeps." Ernie sat back.

"What's the address?" Mason kept his features neutral while his brain tossed questions and answers back and forth.

Ernie slid the paper across to Mason. "Something else…they were kinda weird. Just before they left I went to play pool with a friend, and they were deep in conversation. They weren't calling this guy their boss. They called him *savior*."

"How does anyone know to look for you, Mason?" Cara asked as they got back in the car.

"I don't know. I was there when they came to Beth's, but I don't think any of them made it back to tell the tale. Besides, I didn't flash my badge, so nobody should know who I am." Mason started the car and sat back, turning the air on full. South Florida could be brutal in the summer. Wearing a jacket to hide the shoulder holster didn't help.

"Is it even the same guy? Are you working on anything else? How about Dizzazio, could it be him?" Cara took off her jacket and tossed it to the back seat.

"I might have thought so if not for that last remark. Savior? Dizzazio's men might think a lot of things of him but savior is definitely not one of them. Christian—savior—it fits." Mason pulled into traffic.

"Hang on a second."

Mason tried to keep his eye on her and drive through traffic at the same time. "Please. I've been looking forward to more crappy news."

She turned to him. "I know why we haven't found any bodies drained of blood. Granted, with what little information we have I can't be sure, but my gut tells me it's right. Beth said a vampire doesn't have to kill to feed. There have been about thirty odd disappearances in the last month. What if they're not victims, but volunteers?" Cara twisted in her seat to look at Mason.

"You mean he didn't want to leave any bodies to cause suspicion, so he keeps his meals around by getting them to believe he's the Messiah ready for His Second Coming? That would be okay, but what about the whole biting thing. Far as I know, Jesus never bit anyone."

"True, but Beth also said that the experience didn't have to be painful; in fact, a vampire can make it euphoric. If he did it right he could pass it off as spiritual. He's got powers, Mason; he could convince people he is something other than what he is. If he's got innocent people hoodwinked into believing he's the savior, imagine how far they'll go to protect him when we go after him."

"How far would you go to stand up for God?"

"I don't want to have to go through thirty innocent people to get to him, Mason, or even better have them come after us to get the book and the ring."

"Let's hope it doesn't get that far." Mason looked at the cross that swung from his mirror and prayed he wouldn't have to make the choice.

CHAPTER 30

Cara called Beth, gave her the address they were headed to, and explained how they had gotten their information.

"Can't Mason call in some backup?" Beth wished that she could go and protect Cara, but she knew better than to even suggest it. The powers that be wanted her right where she was.

"And tell them what? Officer needs assistance with a vampire that is passing himself off as the Son of God?"

"Run that by me again. He's doing what?" Beth stood up and paced her living room.

Cara relayed her idea.

"It makes sense. All types of creatures have tried to pass themselves off as Gods to humans for centuries." Beth's heart pounded when she realized that this might be it, the showdown they had all been anticipating. "At least call Thomas and have him meet you there."

Cara clicked off and dialed Thomas' cell phone. When he answered she told him everything from their meeting, including what they suspected and where they were headed.

"Hold on, we're just wrapping up here. Let me tell Jonathan." He was back on the phone in an instant. "I'm going to meet you there. We'll keep an eye on the place, and when Jonathan can get away he'll meet us there. Do not go in!"

"Bring something big and sharp," Cara replied.

"No worries there." Thomas clicked off.

Jonathan was just shutting the door behind the police when Thomas returned his phone to his pocket.

Thomas moved to Jonathan's wall unit, reached in, and hit a button. The unit swung away from him and he walked through the opening and into a large room lined with cabinets; some held weapons, others held rare books in ancient languages. It was here that Jonathan researched the book he had taken from Christian long ago. Thomas removed his jacket and took a half sword from the cabinet. He put on a custom sheath that allowed him to hide it behind his back. He grabbed a trench coat from a small closet and put a full sword inside it, hidden in the lining. Jonathan watched him with hooded eyes from the doorway.

"We both know this is a set up." He moved away from the door and back towards his office.

"Cara and Mason know it, too. But I don't see that we have much choice." Thomas exited the hidden room and secured it. "We've got to find Christian soon, even if it is on his own turf. We can't wait this out with Christian killing everything in sight. I've got more teams on the streets but we've lost some men and the attacks are getting worse."

"Don't go in without me," Jonathan warned.

"We won't." Thomas could see the impatience straining in Jonathan. The rage was just barely under the surface, intensified by the fact that he had to wait until sundown. No matter how human he could make himself appear, he was still chained to the night.

Thomas glanced at the desk where Valerie's body had been found earlier that day and clamped his teeth together. Somebody was going to pay.

Cara and Mason turned the corner in their car and made their way down the isolated street. It was deserted.

"I know these buildings have been empty for a while," said Mason, "but I came to a Panther game here with Cathy before they moved the stadium, and there were people everywhere. This spot was a particular favorite of the homeless. Christian's attacks even have the homeless off the streets." Mason slowed the car as Cara looked for building numbers. Satisfied, he stopped the vehicle in the middle of the block and turned off the engine. "It should be right down at the end. We're still going to wait for the other two to get here, I take it?"

"I would like to get the show on the road myself, but I'd also like to come out of there in one piece." Cara checked her weapons, then shoved two clips in each back pocket. She looked down the block; not a soul in sight. "Maybe we should at least have a look around. Make sure there's no way they can slip out or in without us knowing."

"We'd have to split up." Mason shifted in the seat to look at her.

"Where's your sense of adventure?" She smiled and opened the door.

They met around at the trunk and Mason took out two radios and handed her one. "If you don't answer I will come shooting and find out why later." Mason took his jacket off. It didn't look like there was anyone to question why he was walking around heavily armed. "I'll take the back. You take the front."

Mason slid between the buildings to head for the back as Cara walked down the block. She thought back to the night that had started all of this and hoped that Mason wouldn't meet the same end Danny had. When she reached the front of the building she could see that the windows had all been blacked out. No sign could tell her what kind of establishment had been here. She could hear muffled noises from inside. *Hmm, they're already here.*

"Cara, one exit back here." Mason's voice came over the radio. "I hear movement, but I can't make out any specifics."

"I hear it too, I—" Cara's voice was cut off as a scream from inside the building pierced the silence. She could feel the terror coming through the door in waves.

"Going in."

She threw the radio to the ground and tried the door. It was locked. She armed herself with both guns, used one to fire a bullet at the lock, then kicked the door open. The only thing to fire at was Mason bursting through the back door. They stopped, scanning the empty building. Mason crossed the room to her.

"I heard a scream. Some type of recording?"

"No, she's here and she's terrified. I feel her." Cara scanned the room again. She spotted a door at the far corner and headed toward it. "Up," she said.

"Remember we are probably dealing with volunteers, not victims. She could be leading us up there." Even as Mason said it he followed her.

"You can't fake horror like this." Cara shoved one of her guns into the back of her jeans and Mason covered her while she yanked the door open and plastered herself against the wall. A dark staircase led up to a faint light at the top.

Cara took her second gun back out and started up the staircase. Mason followed, keeping an eye on the stairs behind them. Cara reflected briefly that she should have practiced firing with both guns. One was slightly heavier than the other, but there was no time to worry about it now.

Almost to the top. Shit, another closed door. The woman's fear was so strong now that Cara could feel it battering against her. She drew it into her like a breath, trying to find clarity and understanding from the emotion rather than fighting it. She cleared her mind, nodded to Mason, took a step back, and kicked the door in.

Cara went immediately to her knee as Mason came over the top of her. She took a split second to orient herself to the room, her thoughts registering the situation in parallel, no other exits, ten vamps, woman bleeding, blood everywhere.

The vampires descended in a rush, like bats fleeing a cave. Only their target wasn't escape, it was Cara and Mason. Conscious of her developing abilities, Cara let out a primal scream and with it every emotion she had been holding in—the woman's horror, her anger—surged forward, and the vampires ran smack into the resulting wall. It didn't stop them for long, but their momentum was gone and they were confused.

Methodically, Cara and Mason began firing. Two went down shrieking in pain, disbelieving they couldn't immediately spring up. Two more kept coming right at Cara and Mason, while others closed in on their sides. They fanned out their shots, targeting hearts, but they were happy with any hits.

By hugging the wall, one short but well-muscled vampire got close enough to Cara to land a kick to her shoulder from the side, knocking her against the door frame and into the room. Instinctively she landed and rolled, popping right back up onto her knees, but in the process one of her guns clattered to the floor. Mason leapt through the door, kicked her fallen weapon in her direction, then covered her while she retrieved and reloaded the gun. Then it was his turn to reload in the sort of semi choreographed chaos that engulfed the room. Vampires, especially when angry, move much faster than humans; though both Cara and Mason had become aware of that fact in their first fight with them. Making the adjustment in the middle of a hurricane-like attack on their lives was an incredible challenge.

In the melee, one of the vamps that had gone down squirmed his way close enough to lunge forward and grab Mason's ankle, jerking him to floor. Cara took a quick jump forward, kicked the vampire squarely in the face to drive his nasal bones into his cranium, then fired right into his mangled features. Another vampire immediately sprang into the vacated space behind her, grabbing her by the hair. She brought her gun across her body and jammed it into his stomach, firing twice. Then her gun clicked empty.

Though wounded and hurting, the vampire spun her around and backhanded her into the wall. Mason scrambled to his feet just in time to get jumped from both sides. He crashed face first into the middle of the room, and the sharp knee of one of his attackers smashed viciously into the small of his back, driving the wind out of his chest and pinning him to the ground. The other jerked his head to the side and snarled, "You won't want to miss this, pretty boy!"

One vampire grabbed Cara's hands, another her feet, and they dropped her to the floor. A third jumped down to straddle her midsection and yanked her head to the side. Grinning, first at Cara and then Mason, he bared his fangs and laughed before turning back to Cara and descending to her bared and throbbing neck.

CHAPTER 31

Thomas pulled up and parked behind Mason's car. Dread filled him as he scanned the area and didn't spot either of them. He grabbed his cell phone and dialed Jonathan at the office. He didn't wait for a hello. "I'm outside, but they're not here. Car's empty."

"Fuck. If they're not dead, I'm going to kill them both."

Thomas heard Jonathan pick up and throw into the wall what sounded like a pencil holder, followed by what sounded like Jonathan clearing the top of a desk of its contents. As Thomas listened to Jonathan destroy his office, he got out of the car.

A shot rang out, and Thomas yelled, "Shit!" as he dropped the phone and took off at top speed down the block. He thought he heard Cara scream, it must have been her voice. He redoubled his efforts. At the front door he slowed only long enough to see that the lock had been blown to smithereens as the air filled with the rapid staccato of handguns mingled with the howling of wounded vampires. As he ran toward the noise and the staircase that led to it, he reached behind his back and slid the short sword from its scabbard. Just as he reached the staircase, everything went quiet.

As he started up the stairs, he heard a laugh and bounded up three steps at a time. Almost at the top, the silence was broken again.

"*No!*" Mason's scream held a mixture of anger, disbelief, terror, and ultimate anguish, all blending to stop Thomas' heart mid beat. He flew to the landing, the door stood open. Five vampires were huddled in the corner nursing wounds, one was trying his best to hold his face together. A woman Thomas did not recognize cowered against the far wall, sobbing into her sleeve as she held her arm protectively over her face. Cara and Mason were on the floor, held by the others. Cara's face was obscured by a rather large vampire descending upon her neck. Thomas snatched out his second sword and went to war.

His first victim was the son of a bitch sitting on top of Cara. With a yell and a swing powered by years of anger, he cut his head clean off. The vampire holding Cara's hands watched in horror as it bounced across the floor. That was the last thing he ever saw, as Thomas reversed direction and slashed savagely with the short sword. The Vamp's head sat in astonishment on his shoulders for just a second then fell to the ground as Cara shoved backward on his chest with all her might.

As Thomas went to work on the thugs holding Mason, he saw Cara in his peripheral view as she drew her legs up and kicked the stunned vampire at her feet. She rolled across the floor, grabbed her discarded weapons, reloaded, and started firing. Thomas freed Mason, then tossed him the short sword and pointed to the wounded group in the corner.

They did indeed work well together. In a matter of minutes there were ten decapitated bodies. Sometime in the foray the woman had fled. The three warriors stood gasping; adrenaline still pumping hard. Thomas looked around.

Cara backed up to the wall and leaned against it. "Are we done?" she panted.

Thomas counted heads. "Yeah, we're done."

"Goody," Cara said as her eyes closed and she slid to the floor.

"Shit!" Mason and Thomas cursed in unison as they rushed forward to catch her. Mason carried Cara out of the building while Thomas tore open a boarded-over window and let the waning sunlight do its job on the vamps. Thomas wanted to take her to the hospital, but Cara woke up long enough to tell him that she would shoot him if he didn't take her straight to Beth's. Mason shrugged, got in, and started the car. Thomas picked up his battered phone and drove behind Mason. Luckily, though badly dented, there was enough left of his phone to call Jonathan.

Thomas didn't bother with preamble. "We're all alive."

"I'm calling Cara, I'll call you back."

"Uh, hang on," Thomas stuttered.

"What?"

Thomas relayed what he had walked in on.

"She refused to go to the hospital?"

"She threatened to shoot me." Thomas was grinning. He was really beginning to like Cara, despite her earlier promise to do exactly what she had jokingly threatened.

"I'll meet you at Beth's."

CHAPTER 32

B eth was standing with the door open when Mason and Thomas pulled up. She gasped when Mason carried Cara into the house. Thomas followed them in, then pulled Beth inside behind him. "She'll be okay."

Thomas didn't get to comfort Beth for long; she ushered Mason and his cargo promptly into the nearest bedroom. Then Mason hopped out, got the first aid kit from the kitchen, and disappeared back into the bedroom. For about five seconds Thomas was left feeling like an outsider, until Beth pushed Mason out of the room and slammed the door behind him.

"You'd think I was a peeping tom or something." Mason glared at the closed door.

Thomas laughed. Mason turned to look at him, his face changing. Thomas sobered, not sure what the look meant.

"Thank you, Thomas. I mean it." Mason walked to Thomas and put out his hand.

"You're welcome." They shook.

"Let's get our gear. I don't know about you, but I'm a little sticky," Mason grinned as he headed to the car to get his bag.

After showering, Mason walked barefoot into the living room. Thomas was standing awkwardly in the middle of the room, feeling unsure he should even be there.

"Want a beer?" Mason called to him. "I knew Beth wouldn't have any, so I stopped this morning with Cara on our way to meet our man from the street. We shouldn't drink enough to get loopy, but no harm in a couple."

"Sure." Thomas easily caught the can Mason tossed at him.

"They come out yet?" Mason opened his can and took a long swallow.

"Yeah, Cara came out to take a shower. She doesn't look good. I still think we should have taken her to the hospital." Thomas sat on the arm of a chair.

"Are you *that* anxious to get out of that body?"

Thomas' head whipped to Mason, but when he saw Mason's smile he knew he was just yanking his chain. Thomas relaxed and laughed.

When Cara and Beth came out of the room, Cara's neck was bandaged, she was pale, and her tank top didn't cover the bruising on her shoulder or around her wrists.

"Are you okay?" Thomas asked as he rose.

"I'll be fine." Cara managed a smile before she sank into the couch.

"Jonathan should be here any minute. I'll warn you, he's not happy that you guys went in without waiting." Thomas resumed his seat, and Beth sat beside Cara.

"We didn't have much choice." Cara filled him in on the part he missed.

"I understand you're trained to protect and rescue others, but that's not going to make him any happier." Thomas glanced at Beth. She seemed quiet. When Jonathan knocked on the door a few minutes later, Thomas looked at Beth again. She usually warned them when someone was coming, even if they were harmless. Right know he was holding his breath for the explosion. He got up to answer the door, but only made it halfway there before it opened. Jonathan took one look at Cara and lost it.

"What the fuck did you think you were doing? I told you to wait." Cara didn't respond, but Mason did. He sprung up from the chair and got right in Jonathan's face.

"She did her job. There was someone in that building being torn apart. Neither one of us was going to stand outside that door and listen to a woman screaming her guts out just because you told us to wait." Mason accented the *you* by planting a quick jab with his hand on Jonathan's chest.

Jonathan responded by planting one of his own in Mason's chest, only Mason was shoved back a few feet. He sucked in his breath, and blood began seeping through his shirt. Everyone jumped to their feet, even Sheena from her place beneath the kitchen table, but Thomas stepped in between and faced Jonathan.

"Back off!" Thomas said between his teeth.

"Switching sides?" Jonathan's tone was condescending.

"I know it was hard for you to sit and wait, but don't take out your frustration on us. We haven't had the best day, in case you haven't noticed."

Jonathan looked at Cara's wounds. "I can tell." Anger visibly faded from him. He walked over to Mason and apologized, and the two women settled back down on the couch. Beth's wolf took up a position on a throw rug next to the front door.

"I would have felt the same way if I couldn't do anything to help," Thomas said.

Beth made a small noise, got up from the couch, and excused herself to the bedroom.

Thomas watched her go and started to follow.

"Give her some time to herself. Come on, Mason, let's get you patched up." Cara still hadn't looked at Jonathan.

"I'll do it. You sit down." When Cara remained standing with her back to him, Jonathan added, "Please."

Cara went back to the couch.

"Ouch!" chimed Jonathan and Thomas when Mason gingerly pulled his polo shirt over his head revealing scratches that didn't require stitches, but looked painful nonetheless.

"If you think I look bad—" Mason stopped when Thomas rolled his eyes. "Okay, okay." Mason threw up his hands in surrender, sat down, and Jonathan started to dress the wounds, beginning with the ones he had just reopened when he thumped Mason on the chest. Having just showered, Mason had saved them the trouble of cleaning the wounds first.

"Someone please tell me what went on while I was pacing about my office like a wild animal this afternoon!"

As Mason told the tale, Thomas went to the kitchen and found something to make for dinner. He figured that under the circumstances, Beth would allow him into her kitchen, especially to do nothing more than open some cans of hearty soup and put together a few sandwiches.

As Mason's voice droned on, occasionally punctuated by Cara's corrections, instinctively all of their eyes began to cast about, glancing out Beth's new windows. Their ears also perked up for unusual noises. They all knew it was sundown and they all knew something would happen soon, yet they all maintained that certain surface casualness that seasoned veterans of battle get right before they walk into hell. To the casual observer, they would have looked like friends getting together for an evening, were it not for the fact that no one had less than two weapons within arm's reach.

Dinner was simple. Thomas had kept the fare substantial enough to regenerate fallen energy levels but light enough not to weigh anyone down. Beth recovered enough to join in the conversation, she had the book with her still deciphering it. Thomas kept a watchful eye on her and saw the moment when her laughter stopped and anger spread across her face.

"That bitch!" Beth dropped the book on the table and rushed from the room, leaving everyone staring in astonishment.

CHAPTER 33

A split second after Beth left, Thomas grabbed for his weapons with everyone else in a mad dash to follow her to the front door. She won the race and flung it open. The sun wasn't quite down, and Jonathan had to lunge back to avoid the last stray rays that made their way through the trees. Thomas watched as a black van with darkened windows approached.

"Beth?" Thomas almost whispered. He had seen her angry before, but now her violet eyes glowed and her whole body seemed to be humming.

"Is it her?" Cara asked.

"Yes." Beth's voice was harsh and almost unrecognizable.

"What do we do?" Cara slowly walked to her friend and leaned into her as if she were absorbing the angry waves emanating from within her little body.

"We do whatever we have to."

"Who is it?" Thomas asked louder this time.

"Cavannah. You wanted a bad witch, Thomas. Well, here she comes now." Beth pointed to the van.

"What about the governors?" Cara lowered her voice, but Thomas still caught it.

"She came here even though I'm off limits. She gets whatever she gets. Christian knew he couldn't get through my shields, so he brought something to distract me. Everybody get ready. The shields won't be strong, and if I don't take her out quickly enough they might dissolve altogether." Beth looked at the now motionless van in front of her house. "I may not be able to protect you." Beth's voice broke.

Thomas stepped beside her, took her by the shoulders, and shook her slightly.

"We don't need your protection, just concentrate on getting rid of her, and we'll handle ourselves." His voice offered no argument.

Beth looked at all of them in turn. Then she turned back to the van and her face hardened.

"I'll take care of her." Before Thomas could blink, Beth took off at a run. She cleared the front door and was across the front landing before anyone could stop her.

Cara was the first to try and follow Beth, but she didn't make it past the door. She couldn't, as if the door were shut tight and dead bolted instead of standing wide open. Sheena threw herself repeatedly against the barrier, growling and snapping.

"Oh, God! No!" Cara turned terrified eyes toward the group. "She's blocked us in." Cara turned again and beat against the invisible wall with her fists. Struck dumb by the outburst of emotion from Cara, no one moved for a moment. Then reality set in and Jonathan pulled Cara from the door.

"They'll tear her apart," Cara whispered as she took handfuls of Jonathan's shirt.

Jonathan held her close as Thomas watched Beth reach the van. Cavannah stepped out and shut the door quickly, her companions inside wouldn't care for the amount of light still lingering. She was tall and slim, and while her face was not unattractive, the expression of dissatisfaction that continually crossed her thin sharp features gave her a pinched look. At this moment however an actual smile hovered on her lips.

Thomas watched Beth moving in on the van and wondered if he would ever get the chance to tell her how wrong he had been.

Beth stopped when Cavannah faced her, throwing both hands in front of her. A visible energy shot out from Beth, catching Cavannah in the midsection and slamming her into the van. Beth reached for the slim witch with bare hands and grabbed her by the hair, dragging her away from the van. If she couldn't get rid of Cavannah by the time the sun was completely down, she wanted to be able to move easily back into the house. She could use Mason's ability, but only as a last resort.

By catching her enemy by surprise, she almost made it to the house when Cavannah grabbed the hands tangled in her hair. Beth let out a scream as she spun through the air and collided with the house. They rose and faced each other. Beth could feel the gash in her shoulder from the stones, but brushed it aside. Cavannah circled Beth. Beth stood still and drew in a breath, gathering her power around her. She felt it like electricity through her body. The white glow that seemed to follow Beth's power shimmered around her.

Cavannah struck out with her own power in a savage lash. It slapped against Beth's white glow, and the little woman tossed her hand like a horse flipping off a fly with its tail. Beth's energy flew back along the line of power Cavannah had unleashed, and before Cavannah could stop it, the backlash whipped through her body. Stunned and smarting, she turned to the door of Beth's house.

The greenish glow that accompanied Cavannah's power grew again and again; she tossed a lash of it toward Beth, but this time while Beth repelled it, Cavannah whipped her power at the house and Beth's shields around her home shattered. Beth felt it and redoubled her attack on Cavannah, driving her to her knees. Then she heard a click behind her and turned in time to see the sliding door on the van open. She looked at the sky. The sun was gone.

As Beth's shields fell, Cara was the first out the door, the others right at her back. Vampires spilled from the van, they must have been sitting on top of one another: six, seven, eight . . . Beth stopped counting and spread her hands, holding her head to the heavens. Light spilled from her and spread across the lawn, encompassing her allies. The vampires shrank back toward the van.

Jonathan changed as he closed the distance to the van; he passed Beth in a blur as the light she emitted drifted back from him as he raced on. He had no weapons, but blood began to spill nonetheless. His fury unleashed itself in a whirl of motion. Beth knew he could not kill them, but he could injure and maim, leaving the killing blow to the others. Bullets and swords clashed with flesh. Fangs and claws reached out, slashed, and drew blood.

Beth watched Cavannah flee into the trees, as one by one her vampire companions were flayed and decapitated.

CHAPTER 34

The five of them stood panting, slightly dazed with the rush of action. Even Sheena lay down next to Beth, having given every ounce of energy in defense of her master. The yard was littered with bodies. Jonathan walked toward the trees, separating himself from the others. Thomas motioned for everyone to move inside. Cara didn't follow but waited, staring at Jonathan's back. Thomas started to say something but must have changed his mind because he went inside with everyone else. Cara approached Jonathan and ran her hand down his back.

"Go away." Jonathan's voice was low and hoarse.

"Why?" Cara walked around to face him and he turned from her. "Don't turn your back on me."

"You want to see the *monster?* Is that it? Well, take a good look, Cara!" He yelled at her as he turned to face her. She had seen him bare his teeth before, but this was new to her. His skin was pale, his eyes completely black. None of the brilliant blue could be seen. Claws pushed from his fingers, almost obscured by the blood that clung to them. Oh, the blood, it was everywhere, splattered across his face, drenching the front of his shirt, dripping from his hands and forearms. "I need a moment." He sounded like he was trying to inject some civility into his tone, but it was still close to a growl.

"I want to help." Cara stared at him.

"You can't help with this."

Cara stood uncertain. She wasn't afraid of him but for him. She stepped closer and took his face in her hands.

Her touch ignited something in him and he grabbed her wrists and dragged her easily into the forest. After a few feet he stopped and swung her around to him.

"Do you want me like this, Cara?" Jonathan pushed her up against a tree and leaned into her body.

"Are you trying to see how far you can push me?" she replied. "See if you can push me away totally? You can't." As she said it she took his face again, pulling his lips down to her mouth. She could feel the control break, the rush of lust pour through him. Their clothes were gone before she could take a breath. Jonathan's mouth streaked over her almost too fast for her body to recognize the sensations, but there was no mistaking the animal that pulsed in him, the dark passion that surged forward for satisfaction, and she used it. She pulled it inside, added her own need, and pushed it back at him. He stopped and stared at her, then shook his head as if trying to clear it. But Cara didn't want him to have his control back; she took advantage of his hesitation by slipping her hand around what hardened between them. He steadied himself by holding her shoulders. As she massaged him, his grip tightened. His nails had not fully retracted and a small cut appeared above the swell of her breast where his thumb pressed. His gaze zeroed in on it and Cara felt the hunger for it whip through her.

She whispered, "Take it," and quickly felt the ground beneath her back before Jonathan slid inside of her. She saw him lower to the cut below her shoulder; his tongue flicked out and licked it. The pleasure of it shot through her.

He took her roughly, entering her body over and over again, as fully as he could each time. It wasn't enough. She wanted more. He lifted her legs higher, went faster. When her climax exploded around him, he didn't stop. Bending down he sucked her wound, and his whole body tightened with demand. He brought her up again and when she cried out his name, arching her back off the ground, his body spasmed as he came.

They lay there tangled together for some time.

"Did I hurt you?" Jonathan asked gently as he rolled off of her onto his back, yet keeping one hand splayed across her stomach as if he were afraid the moment she was free of his weight she might run away.

"Am I still alive?" Cara turned to look at Jonathan through half-closed eyes.

"Don't be cute, and don't ever push me like that again. I could have hurt you. I could have killed you." Jonathan's voice was low and pained.

"No, no you couldn't have. Maybe you weren't able to tell, but I felt it the moment all control broke, the moment the hunger took over. You still didn't attack me. You're not a monster, no matter what you've convinced yourself of. Jonathan the human doesn't kill for hunger; Jonathan the vampire wouldn't either." Cara stood and began dressing and picking leaves out of her hair.

"I am a killer, Cara. Do not be mistaken about that." Jonathan sat up but made no move to dress. "I could have killed today if I wasn't afraid of leaving the rest of you unprotected when Christian finally makes his move."

"I killed both today and yesterday. What does that make me?" she asked.

"I'm not talking about self defense." He slowly stood to dress.

"Who were they?" Cara asked serenely as she grabbed her weapons and watched him dress.

"What do you mean?"

"Are there hundreds of innocent virgins buried somewhere?"

"No!" Jonathan looked horrified. "I could go without for months. I had only been turned for ten years when I discovered there was no need to kill. Nobody I ever took was innocent. Not by a long shot."

"Oh yeah, you're a regular fiend, aren't you. Feeling guilty over the miserable lives you had to take to survive. Protecting your friends, no matter the cost to yourself. I can see where you get the monster idea." Cara turned and headed back to the house, shaking her head at his inability to see what a good man he was.

CHAPTER 35

Thomas shut the door and wondered whether it was wise to let Cara head into the woods after Jonathan. He had seen Jonathan when changed and he was not always in top form. Leaving them to their own devices, he in turn went in search of Beth, intent on getting some answers from her. He found her in the library, where she sat with her head resting on folded arms. He walked quietly to her and bent down beside her.

"Are you okay?" Thomas didn't believe her when she nodded without lifting her head. "If you think you'll get out of a lecture on the stupidity of rushing out the door without us by coming in here and pouting, you're wrong."

"I don't pout. I'm mad. She got away." Beth lifted her head and rested her chin on her arms.

"We're all alive, Beth. I think we should be thankful for that. And we owe you a great deal of credit. But if you ever pull a stunt like that again I'll make sure, if you're still alive, that you'll regret it." His voice started out light but ended on a rough note.

"I did what I thought was best. I can't do you any good anywhere else but here. When you're here I can protect all of you, so why shouldn't I?"

"Why not?" Now he was getting to the subject he'd been wondering about.

"Why not what?" Beth sat up a little straighter.

Thomas maneuvered her right where he wanted her. "Why don't you leave here? The first time I saw you was when I followed Cara here. You were obviously happy to see her, but you didn't rush out to greet her." Thomas looked away. "When I asked you out for dinner, you declined but said we could eat here. You could have helped Mason and Cara yesterday, but you didn't. You don't ever seem to leave this house, Beth. Why is that?"

Beth stared at him like she was wondering how to answer. "Remember when we spoke about secrets? This is mine."

"My secret almost got me zapped, Beth. How about yours?" Thomas stood and looked down at her. He wanted so badly to trust her, to be able to follow through on the attraction that hadn't abated even when he found out that she was a witch. But she wasn't giving an inch.

"Mine won't get me killed. Besides, I left tonight when Cavannah came." Beth raised her eyes and met his.

"I have the feeling that was an exception. I also get the feeling that you're not going to explain what's between you and Cavannah." He caught the tell tale flicker in her eyes. Thomas stared at her for another moment, giving her the chance to confide in him. She said nothing. He turned to walk out of the library.

"She okay?" Mason asked Thomas as they entered the living room at the same time.

"Huh? Oh, yeah."

"Good. She hit that wall pretty hard. She must be tougher than she looks."

Thomas looked up at Mason and replayed the scene in his mind. He'd been so concerned with getting his answers, he hadn't even thought about her being injured. He spun on his heel without saying anything to Mason and went back to the library.

"Where are you hurt?" Thomas found Beth as she was the first time he came in, but her head came up at his question.

"I'm fine."

"Bullshit." Thomas walked behind her. The back of her shirt was torn and dirty. He could see the flesh beneath it and the blood. "I want to look at that back."

Beth dug in her heels when Thomas took her hand to lead her from the room. She tried to yank her hand away but sucked in a quick breath. "You're hurting me."

"If you would come on and let me look at it, I wouldn't be hurting you."

"I'll wait for Cara."

"Cara went after Jonathan. I don't know how long she'll be. It's best if you let me treat it now." Thomas quit pulling her but didn't let go of her hand.

"Fine."

Thomas led her to her bedroom, grabbing the first aid kit on the way. They had all come to appreciate that first aid kit over the last few days, and he made a mental note to restock it the next time he went back into the city. Once inside the bedroom, he took a quick look around. He didn't get further than the huge bed that took up most of the room before he started feeling a little uncertain himself.

Thomas set the kit on the bed, cleared his throat, and as firmly as he could he requested, "Take off your shirt."

Beth stared at him for a while before finally turning her back, unbuttoning her shirt, and taking it off.

Thomas watched from the corner of his eye as he opened the kit. He noticed she was shaking slightly. *Probably just reaction setting in,* he thought. *Poor thing, I should have taken care of this earlier.* She pulled her long, flowing hair over the front of her shoulder; as she did he caught a glimpse of her profile. Her white skin made the blush creeping across her face obvious. His stomach did a flip as he thought she might be embarrassed. Thinking he was being stupid, he walked to her dresser and turned on the lamp for more light. As he turned back he caught his first look at her. A four-inch gash dominated her left shoulder; the rest of it was covered in scrapes. Bruising was already altering the color of her skin. He swallowed again as he flashed to her slamming into the wall and to himself questioning her, when he should have been doing what he was doing now. His fingers were gentle when he touched the skin around the wound, but Beth still flinched.

"Sorry," Thomas mumbled.

She stood rigid as he began to clean the dirt away.

Thomas kept his attention focused on what he was doing. If he didn't, he might notice how soft her skin was or how delicate she seemed. He might be distracted by the way she smelled or by the way she seemed to instinctively lean into him. If he didn't concentrate, he might just push her down on her massive bed, and her secrets be damned.

"Beth, I'm sorry, but you'll have to take your bra off." Thomas had cleaned what he could, but the last part of her wound was hidden by her bra, and the movement of the straps was sure to aggravate the injury if not properly attended to.

Beth didn't move.

"It's okay." Thomas brushed his hand along her uninjured shoulder. He was trying to be reassuring.

Beth unhooked it quickly and dropped it to the floor. Thomas turned and retrieved more cleaning solution from the kit. He turned to finish cleaning the injury and stopped dead. He could see her naked breast. *My God, is there nothing about this woman that isn't perfect?* Desire welled up inside, and he whipped his head back around, rummaging through the kit again while trying to clear the image from his head.

Thomas managed to clean the wound out completely. He probably wasn't as gentle as he could have been, his hands were shaking too badly. He was wondering how he was going to apply the butterfly stitches when Cara knocked gently on the door, then came into the room. He whispered a thankful prayer and nearly threw the supplies at her as he walked out the door.

In the hallway he ran into Jonathan who had just opened the door to the bathroom. He had towels in hand, intending to take a shower. Thomas grabbed the towels, pushed passed Jonathan, and slammed the bathroom door. He turned the spray on full and freezing.

CHAPTER 36

Beth's dining room table was littered with maps and files. Based on information trickling in from the station, Mason was still trying to pinpoint an area where Christian might have set up residence. Cara was resting on the couch; Jonathan hovered near her. Beth came out of the library with Jonathan's book.

"Jonathan." Beth looked up when Jonathan didn't answer. All his attention was focused on Cara. Cara was aware of it as she addressed him, "Jonathan, Beth is talking to you. Quit staring at me and answer her."

"I'm sorry, Beth."

"That's okay. Can you fly?" Beth looked excited.

"Pardon me?" Jonathan sounded like maybe he hadn't heard her right, but Cara knew he had excellent hearing.

"Can you fly?"

"You mean am I a pilot?"

"No, I mean can you levitate your body through the air?" Beth pushed.

"No."

"Oh." Beth's face fell.

"Sorry to disappoint. Why?"

"Well, according to this the old ones could fly. I thought it might be neat to see."

"Where did you read that?" Jonathan rose to see the passage Beth was referring to.

"Right here." She turned the book round and showed the room a paragraph made completely of symbols.

"What sort of alphabet is this?" Jonathan took the notebook she held that contained the translation she had made of the paragraph.

"Gargoyle," Beth answered matter-of-factly.

"Gargoyles." Mason's head came up. "Beth, one day you'll have to sit with me and go through what's real and what's not." Mason shook his head.

"Have you been able to find anything that could tell us how many we might be up against?" Jonathan handed Beth back her notebook.

"Not yet," she answered as she turned to go back to her library and her translation work.

Thomas entered the living room and went to help Mason with the map.

"I've been thinking," Cara said carefully as she rose to a sitting position. The tone in her voice was enough to make Beth turn back from her path to the library and listen. "What if you turned us all, except Thomas?" Cara steeled herself for an explosion, which, of course, she got.

Nearly everyone spoke, or rather yelled, at once. There was a range of expletives used. Beth however was quiet, she seemed to be considering it. Cara raised her hands for silence.

"Did someone hit you in the head tonight?" Mason had left his maps and stood across from Cara.

"No."

"Then maybe someone should!"

"I second that motion," Thomas said, although Cara figured it wouldn't affect him.

"I think the idea has merit, but I don't know what it would do to me. I'm sure I have a book that covers it." Beth looked around at the faces giving her slightly astounded expressions.

"There is nothing you could say that would convince me to change any of you! That's final!" Jonathan turned his back on everyone, as if he were a child who thought that no one could speak if he couldn't see them.

150

"Just listen." Cara waited until Jonathan turned around. The anger on his face made her hesitate, but she forged ahead. "We would have a better chance of surviving this."

"I'm all for living, Cara, but don't you think that's extreme?" Mason leaned forward. "Living forever isn't exactly my cup of tea."

"Christian wouldn't be able to kill any of us," Cara was warming to her subject.

"Ah, but you wouldn't be able to kill him either," Jonathan noted.

"No, but if we get him, Thomas could."

Cara looked at Thomas who was startled and replied, "Not that I don't love the idea, but I agree with Mason, it's a little extreme."

"Cara, there is no guarantee that what you changed into would be remotely close to what you are now," explained Jonathan.

"I thought about that, too. I can't believe that Christian would change anyone without being sure that he could use him for murder and mayhem. Take you, for example; when he changed you, he didn't mean to, but once you turned he couldn't get rid of you. I believe that if you're a good person, you change to, well, a good vampire."

"You didn't volunteer?" This from Mason. He wasn't privy to the information Cara had. She knew he already had a grudging respect for Jonathan but finding out he didn't choose to be what he was probably bumped him up a notch.

"It's not a temporary thing, Cara. Are you going to spend eternity as a vampire just to rid yourself of Christian?" Jonathan looked at Beth. "Do you really think you could hunt for victims?"

"No, but you don't hunt either, you own a blood bank, right?" commented Cara. He gave her a nasty look. "If you don't like the idea, forget it. I thought it would give us an edge. We don't have the advantage of being practically immortal or choosing a new body when it's time to move on. Pardon the fuck out of me!" She stormed outside.

God, what's the matter with me? I never lose my temper like that. She noticed her hands were shaking. *Oh shit, not now.* She thought that with the way she was using her emotional power, she could keep from having these backlashes. The trembling traveled up her arms. She found a seat on Beth's patio and waited for it to subside.

Jonathan found her on the patio, by which time she was shaking from head to foot. He knelt down in front of her. "What's wrong?" His voice revealed his concern.

Cara shook her head and tried to wave him away, but he picked her up like a child and sat in the chair with her on his lap.

"Go away," her voice shook.

"No." Jonathan held her tightly until the trembling stopped. "Talk to me."

"It happens sometimes. I can only hold so much and then it just overflows. I thought it would go away. I've been using the emotions, pushing them out. I don't understand." She laid her head on Jonathan's shoulder.

"You normally live alone. You have a place to go where no one's feelings can get to you. Since this started, you've been absorbing everyone's tension, fear, whatever."

"I guess you're right."

They sat quietly for a while.

"Cara," Jonathan said softly. "I'd like to have more of this when our lives are normal again."

"What kind of life would we have?"

"You could move into the apartment; if you don't like it there, we could find someplace else. More time like this, quiet and content. Passion. Love."

"Love?" Cara's heart skipped at the word. "For how long?"

"Forever," Jonathan whispered against her ear, sending goose bumps down her arms.

"No, not forever. You have forever. I have maybe sixty some odd years left. I don't know if I want you to watch me grow old. I've known you for a week, and these are the questions I'm asking myself. I'm thinking of all the women you'll have after I'm gone, and I'm jealous. I don't like it, not any of it."

"Is that what the turning argument was about?"

"Maybe."

"Are you saying that if I don't turn you, after this is over, you won't see me?" His question was deadly soft.

"I'm not sure."

"When you have an answer, be sure to let me know." Jonathan got up and set her in the chair. He rounded the corner of the house and had nearly disappeared when he turned around.

She had folded herself so that her head rested on her knees. She was crying and it seemed to startle him.

"I'm sorry." Cara was mortified. "I never cry. I just don't know what to do. I always know what to do."

"I know the feeling. We'll figure it out."

Cara sniffled once more and wiped her eyes with her sleeve.

"I bet if I keep crying, you'll do anything I want. You look a little panicked."

"I don't panic."

"Yeah, right."

CHAPTER 37

Beth sat at her table and studied the book again. She'd cross checked and translated, researched and re-read, but still felt she was missing something. She'd thought she'd had it but when the calculations were finished the date made no sense at all. There were still passages that needed to be deciphered but she was sure they weren't affecting the outcome of the date. Beth had a crushing feeling she was going to fail.

She lowered her head to the table, whether it was from fatigue or defeat she was unsure.

"Beth," Thomas said quietly. She raised her head, feeling tired and beaten. "It'll be okay."

"No, it won't. It won't ever be right Thomas. This," she shoved the notebook toward him, "is all I can do. Play with my books and papers and right now I can't even do that."

Thomas hated the despair in her voice. "Listen," he sharpened his voice. "The Ancient came to you because you had the knowledge to figure this out. He *knew* you could do it." His words seemed to break through the shell of desperation that cloaked her.

"Thank you, Thomas," she replied with a soft smile and Thomas had to restrain himself from puffing out his chest. This little bit of a woman did the strangest things to him. Beth started to pull the notebooks back toward her. The notebook with her calculations on it had flipped upside down. As she stared at it she frowned.

"What?"

"Oh, oh!" Beth jumped up from the table and ran to the book shelf. She reached for a book that was too high for her. Worried, Thomas followed her and when she turned to get her step stool she smacked into him. "Oh, good. Get that book." She pointed and Thomas reached up. "Ugh, not that one, to the left."

Thomas raised an eyebrow at her impatience and grabbed the book she requested.

"Yes!" she snapped. She went to snatch it from him and he held it out of her reach.

"Are you sure this is the one you want?" Thomas smiled as she jumped for the book.

"Bully," Beth said through gritted teeth before punching him in the stomach, and grabbing the book when he bent over in pain. She returned to the table. "Don't *ever* mess with my books." Beth flipped through it as she reached for the copy she'd made of Jonathan's book. She explained that she made copies so she could make notations and not ruin the ancient artifact, although Jonathan assured her she was welcome to burn it. The look she had given Jonathan at the mention of burning the book said she would sooner set *him* on fire.

Thomas watched now as she flipped more pages, matching up what he assumed were symbols but looked more like chicken scratch.

"Got it!" she yelled and dashed into the living room with Thomas at her heels. Jonathan and Cara were just walking in the door and Mason was watching the news. "August 13, 2010," she called out as they all turned to her. They didn't even have a week.

"I did the original calculations using my latest copy of Darminion Language Uncovered. But the answer I came up with was before Christ was born and I figured that Christian wasn't planning on going back in time, but I rechecked the figures over and over and came up with the same answer. Then Thomas came in and the notebook was upside down and it looked like a date so Thomas got the book and I punched him and," Beth took a breath, slightly lightheaded by the excitement of the discovery.

"Okay Beth, breathe." Cara took the paper from her.

"Okay." Beth started again trying not to sound quite so hysterical.

"I realized that I had a copy of the Darminion Language used ages and ages ago and the new book had tried to modernize some of the meaning, so I looked at my old book and realized my calculations were correct, they were just backwards." She still sounded hysterical. "Forget it, that's the date," Beth said giving up. It was quiet for a moment as Thomas grinned at her. Everyone else looked unsure as to her sanity.

"Anything else?" Cara asked.

"Christian has to have both the book and the Elder ring in order to tap into the power the ancients used to leave this world. He'll be able to make his own rules, make as many vampires as he wishes. We'll be overrun. The way I see it, we have no choice but to stop him completely. Us having the book and the Elder ring has driven him to kill in the open. Can you imagine what he'll do if he thinks he might miss the opportunity he's waited three hundred years for?"

CHAPTER 38

Five-thirty wasn't a whole lot better for bad news. This time when the phone rang, Mason was the recipient. When everyone gathered in the dining room Mason was pacing while on the phone. No one said a word, the look on his face was enough.

"When?" Mason was listening as he put his shoulder holster on. He looked up at Cara, and the misery he was feeling pulled at her. He mouthed to her and she began getting ready.

"What is it?" Jonathan whispered.

"I don't know," Cara answered as she checked her weapons.

"Then why are you leaving with him?"

"Don't worry, I'll make sure you get those sixty or so years." She rose on tiptoe, kissed him, and knew she had managed to shock him again by being affectionate in front of the others.

Mason lowered his cell phone and hung his head. "They're all dead."

"Who?" Cara went to stand beside him, putting a hand on his arm.

"The team I had doing surveillance on Dizzazio." He grabbed his badge. "I want you to go with me, Cara."

"I'm not official right now, Mason."

"You're as official as I say you are." There was steel in his voice. "I don't think this was Dizzazio. I think it was that fuck." He turned and walked out the door. Cara followed leaving the others behind.

"How many?" Cara asked when they got in the car.

"Four."

"Who?"

"Jinkins, Mcgrath, Dean, and Riker."

"Shit, Dean's wife just had a baby a few months ago. I'm sorry, Mason."

"You know what kills me? I couldn't even warn them. I couldn't tell them what they were up against. They might have been able to protect themselves, but I had to keep my mouth shut."

"We're back to how Christian knows you're in with us."

"I can't figure it out. I'm nameless to them."

She thought in silence on the hour drive to Millionaire Mile. The wealthy families that lived there had the advantage of the intracoastal on one side and beach front property on the other. And they paid for it. The locals nicknamed it millionaire mile. The surveillance team had taken over a smaller, mere 1.2 million dollar home to keep watch on Dizzazio. From there they could monitor the listening and visual devices they had planted, and move quickly if need be.

They pulled into the private driveway. Police and emergency vehicles took up most of the space. As Cara walked up the drive, she nudged Mason.

"What?" He looked in the direction she motioned to with her chin and saw Vinton. "I don't have time for him right now. Let's take a look inside, make sure we know who's responsible, and then I'll deal with him."

They walked into the house, stopped at the door, and pulled on thin latex gloves. Cara could see one of the bodies from the front door, but couldn't tell who it was; the corpse seemed to be missing its head. Blood splattered the walls and pooled underneath the body. Walking carefully, they went through the house room by room. The carnage was the same everywhere. Each officer had been taken to a separate room, beaten, and decapitated. When they finished combing the house Cara and Mason joined the search of the grounds. They had yet to locate the heads. The bodies were taken away, forensics was finishing up, and Cara asked Mason to drop her at her apartment while he went to the station. As they set out for the car, Vinton caught them just outside the front door.

"Mason." Vinton looked way too smug to be on the scene where four officers had been savagely mutilated. When a fellow officer goes down, everyone on the force takes it personally.

"Vinton, I'm surprised to see you here, this isn't your case."

"I would think you'd want all the help you could get. Unless you already know who did it." Vinton looked at Cara and raised one eyebrow.

"I have my theories, Vinton, and I always get my man." He walked around Vinton and continued to the car.

"Yeah, Mason, you're quite the savior." Vinton had let Mason go a couple of feet.

"What did you say?" Mason whipped around.

"You're the hero of the department, always so dedicated. Always get what you go after. Did he get you?" He directed the last to Cara, then focused on Mason again. "Better be careful, Mason. Bad things happen to the men in her life."

"Bad things are going to happen to you if you keep this shit up!"

Cara placed her hand on his arm. A warning.

"I'm still young. They say when you're young you think you're immortal," smiled Vinton. "I'm feeling like I could be around for a long time."

Cara and Mason looked at each other.

"How did you know about all this?" Mason motioned toward the house.

"It was on the scanner," Vinton replied.

"No," Mason took a step forward despite Cara trying to hold him back. "We didn't put it on the scanner, you piece of shit. You sold them out."

"I traded," Vinton smiled.

Mason raced across the few feet that separated him from Vinton. Vinton looked surprised when blood spurted from his nose after

Mason landed a right fist into his face. Vinton tried to battle back, but Mason outweighed him, his skills were better, and he was just plain mad enough to kill. Mason kicked Vinton's legs out from under him and knocked him to the ground. He straddled him and began pummeling his face. Cara stood back; she didn't have the strength to remove Mason, and right now she wasn't sure she wanted to if she could. She could feel the anger emanating from Mason, and she didn't know if he would even realize whom he was hitting if she got involved.

Vinton's yells attracted the other officers still around. Cara saw them coming and decided she had better intercede. If she could get him to back off, he might be able to talk his way out of it. If Mason kept beating Vinton when he was no longer able to protect himself, there would be no glossing it over.

She spoke to him before she touched him. Even so he shrugged her off; she stumbled and went at him again. It was too late, the officers rounded the car that had blocked the fight from their view and descended, pulling Mason from Vinton's motionless body. Even though Cara knew that most of them would be secretly thrilled that someone had beaten Vinton senseless, department rules required that they take Mason down to the station. Cara followed in his car.

By the time they arrived, everyone had heard some version of what had happened. Mason was taken directly to the captain's office, while Cara went to her desk by default. It was odd. The only place she'd ever felt she belonged was in the police department, and now she felt strange sitting at her desk.

After a short while, Mason left the captain's office and was accompanied to an interrogation room. The captain stood at the door and watched him go. As he turned to go back into his office, Cara caught his eyes and he motioned her in. When he shut the door behind her, it was none too gently done.

"You wanna tell me what the hell is going on here? I got detectives beating the shit out of each other. One of them, my best. I got another detective on leave at a crime scene where four more officers have been killed, no, mutilated." Captain Monahan sat behind his desk as Cara remained standing. Cara didn't answer; after all, what was she supposed to say? *Technically, sir, Mason is the one who was giving the beating, and Vinton was taking it.*

"Talk to me. Even if it's off the record. I know you know something."

"I have no proof, sir. Anything I say can't leave this room." By the look on the captain's face, she knew she needn't have mentioned it. "Vinton had something to do with the officers being killed today."

She watched that sink in. Monahan had never liked Vinton, but he wouldn't have thought him capable of murdering four cops.

"No proof?" he asked. Cara shook her head. "What were you doing there this morning?"

"Some of the aspects of Danny's murder have been leading into Mason's case. We thought it a good idea to collaborate."

"You're on leave; you're not supposed to be collaborating on anything." When Cara started to say something the captain held up his hand. "Save it. Get me some proof." Just then the captain's phone rang and Cara used the opportunity to slip out.

Mason was released an hour later. Vinton had suffered broken ribs, a broken nose and jaw, and required more than a few stitches. Cara saw Mason coming out and headed to the car.

"Well?" she asked when he got in.

"Suspended until review. Vinton isn't up to pressing charges yet, but I'm sure he will." Mason rested his head on the steering wheel. His knuckles were bruised and swollen with a few scratches.

"No one would blame you if they knew the truth."

"They don't know and they never will."

"I told the captain." At Mason's surprised look she said, "Not everything. I told him we thought Vinton had something to do with the officers who were killed. Off the record." They both knew Monahan would keep it to himself. He would also withhold judgment until he saw solid proof.

Cara's mention of the fallen officers had Mason closing his eyes. "Damn, they were all good men."

"Have the families been notified?"

"Yes. But I should have been the one to do it."

"We'll get them, Mason. We'll get them both."

"Yeah," Mason didn't sound convinced. "Come on, I want to swing by my place. I have a couple things I want to pick up. I'm getting tired of shoving this extra gun in my jeans. They took my piece when they suspended me. I have another at home. I also have a double shoulder holster."

"Do you have two?"

"There's a gun shop on the way. We can stop off," he said pulling the car out.

"Ooh, shopping and weapons. You're the man."

"I'll tell Jonathan you said that." He paused for a second. "You sure you know what you're doing there?"

"No."

"Well, I feel better now."

"Glad I could help." Cara thought about Jonathan as they drove to Mason's. No, she didn't have any idea what she was doing. But she couldn't imagine doing anything else right now.

They stopped at the gun shop and picked up a few goodies. When they got to Mason's, he had Cara come up with him just in case. She followed him around the apartment. She'd never been there before, and it wasn't what she had expected. It was spotless. For a bachelor and a cop that seemed a miracle.

"Do you have a maid?" Cara asked.

"No," Mason smiled as he reached for the closet door. "Oh no! Oh God!"

Cara rushed to Mason to see what was up.

Four heads lined the top shelf of the closet.

CHAPTER 39

Hours passed before Mason and Cara made it back to Beth's as the sun began its descent. There had been no time for phone calls to inform the rest of the group of everything that had transpired. On the drive back Cara didn't speak. There was no teasing Mason out of this mood.

They reached Beth's, unloaded their things from the car, and dragged themselves through the door. Cara immediately dropped her bags and went to Jonathan. He had risen from his chair and folded her into his arms.

Mason set his things by the couch; Beth totally surprised him by walking over and wrapping her arms around him. He settled his arms around the top of her shoulders and rested his head on the top of hers. Then he gave her a squeeze and let her go.

"I needed that."

"I know," Beth smiled sadly and gave him a wink.

She turned to go to the kitchen and Cara caught Thomas scowling at her. When she gave him a quizzical look, he turned away.

Beth had cleared the dining room table, and they sat together as Mason filled them in on their day. When he finished they all sat in silence.

Finally Jonathan spoke up. "It's my fault."

"Did you behead four officers while we were sleeping?"

Jonathan looked amazed that this came from Mason. "No."

"It's not your fault then, is it." This was a statement, not a question.

"At least we know how Christian knew you were in on this," Cara said.

"Now if we could only find the bastard," Mason replied.

"I have an idea on that," Beth spoke up. "If we could convince Christian's men that we had switched locations, you might be able to follow them back to him when they report in."

"How do we do that?" Mason sat up straight.

"You could hide in the woods—" before she could finish Thomas broke in.

"Why wouldn't they search the woods?"

"If you'll let me finish—" She barked at him. "I have a spell that could make you invisible to them. They wouldn't be able to sense Jonathan either."

"How do we follow?" Mason asked. "They might get suspicious if they're followed by a driverless car."

"Hmm." Beth thought for a moment. "Rob. He runs errands for me sometimes and never asks questions."

"Where would you be?" Thomas asked.

"Here."

"You couldn't stay in the house. If they found you, you'd be dead," Mason said. "Why wouldn't you come with us?"

"Don't ask," Thomas said staring at Beth. Cara caught the tension between the two and wondered what she had missed.

"I can use the spell for myself. They won't know I'm here."

They went over the plan several times and finally agreed. Splitting into groups, they checked weapons, and since they had a few hours until sundown, decided to get some sleep. Beth wasn't tired and she wanted to go over the spell one more time so she went to the library.

"This isn't one of those special exceptions, is it?" Thomas startled Beth as he spoke from the doorway. He crossed the room and sat beside her.

"What do you mean?"

"When Cavannah was here and you left the house, it was an exception. Can't you go with us tonight?"

"I can't." Beth's answer was short.

"I'm not prying. I just want to make sure you're safe."

"Sorry." Beth grinned. "What was that look you were giving Mason earlier? I thought you two were okay with each other."

"Nothing." Thomas suddenly found the shelves of the library interesting.

"Was that look for me? Did I do something wrong? I know you don't like me very much, Thomas, but whatever I did I'm sorry." She looked down at her book.

"You didn't do anything." Thomas took a deep breath and plunged ahead. "To be honest, Beth, I do like you. A lot. That's why I gave Mason the look. He had his arms around you and I didn't."

"Oh, um . . ." Beth stared at her book looking way out of her depth.

"It was a shocker for me, too. If I needed a hug, would you give me one?" Thomas leaned toward her and his voice dropped.

Beth turned to find his face close to hers. "Yes."

"Is that all you would give me?

"Depends on what you wanted?"

"Tell me why you won't leave."

"No."

Thomas rose from the chair and went to his room. He lay on the bed wishing he could bite his tongue off. It honestly wasn't what he had planned on saying, but that was what came out. He knew he'd hurt her, but what was he supposed to say? He couldn't shake his need to know. Unfortunately he couldn't shake wanting her either.

Thomas actually had her hoping for something she never thought she'd have, and then he'd snatched it away. Frustrated, she shut the library door. Spells required her full concentration. Their lives depended on her accuracy. Her inner demons would have to wait. Beth read the spell and began to alter it to fit her needs, writing down the changes in her ever present notebook when something brushed against her power. It wasn't pleasant. It felt like someone raked their nails down the inside of her skin.

She rose and reached to find the source. Jonathan's book trembled on the table and Beth dove for it, grabbed it and hugged it to her chest. She heard Mason banging on the door but didn't answer, she couldn't waste her concentration. She slapped at the intruder when she felt a slimy energy creep around the book. Clutching it tighter she felt a second power slide through the room. Splitting her concentration cost her as she was lifted from the ground. She was tossed around, flung across the table and slammed into the book shelf. Holding the book with everything she had, she shot her energy through the room, smashing the second weaker power.

She was picked up again and thrown in the air, crashing into the ceiling. She had to split her power at once fighting the growing malevolence and keeping herself from hurtling to the floor. Beth could hear everyone at the door now. Her books flew from the shelves pummeling her. She sat on the floor curling herself around Jonathan's book, but invisible hands grabbed her by the back of neck and flung her into the wall again. The hands dug into the flesh of her upper arms and rammed her into the wall once, twice, three times then wrapped around her throat. With her airway being crushed, she lost her search for more power and tried to simply breathe. Her vision dimmed and she felt the book being wrenched from her grasp. Finally, she was released and fell to the floor.

She could breathe again and the thing was gone but she hurt everywhere. She couldn't focus as everyone crashed through the door yelling at her. She thought perhaps she was wrong and the thing hadn't left and tried to rise to keep fighting. She made it to her feet and looked around searching for the power, her palms spread as she tried to focus. She swayed as Thomas reached her.

"Oh, God Beth." Thomas' voice sounded so far away. "It's gone. It's okay." Beth tried to stay on her feet but the blackness took her and she collapsed into Thomas' arms.

CHAPTER 40

Mason had been the first to realize that something was wrong, said he'd felt the power and knew it wasn't Beth's. The others had come running when they heard him trying to smash through the library door, screaming for Beth. They had thrown themselves repeatedly at the door and even Jonathan's vampire strength hadn't budged it.

Thomas had thought he knew what it was to be helpless but when he'd heard something tearing apart the library and knew Beth was inside, he was beside himself. He heard her scream several times and some of his sanity left him. They made one more rush at the door and suddenly they were through. They all stopped and stared for a moment at the chaos. Thomas spotted Beth on the floor and all his breath left him. He was frozen as he watched her rise, a bruise already blossoming on the side of her face, and blood trickling from her nose and mouth. He realized as she rose that as battered as she was, she was rising to fight. He moved to her, reassured her that it was over, and caught her as she passed out.

Thomas sat on the couch as Cara looked after Beth. By the time he'd carried her to the bedroom bruises popped out on her arms and her neck, and her hands were raw. After he laid her down he saw his arm covered in blood and knew the wound on her back had opened up. Cara sent him for the kit and then he'd been asked to wait with Mason and Jonathan. They paced. They did not speak. Thomas had almost suggested she go to the hospital, but knew better.

"I've never felt anything like that." Mason dropped into the chair.

"What?" Thomas looked up.

"Whatever was in that room. Evil doesn't even come close. I feel like I need a bath on the inside. I don't know how to explain it."

"We get it." Thomas looked away. Mason hadn't been in the same room with it being tossed around. "Why?"

"Why what?" Mason asked.

"Why did it attack Beth?"

"Because she's the strongest of us, I would imagine." Mason leaned forward bracing his forearms on his knees.

"It didn't go after Beth." Cara came into the room. Thomas thought she looked a little wobbly and then she collapsed on the couch. "She came to when I had to—" Cara broke off and swallowed hard. Thomas couldn't even imagine what she was going to say but he thought he just might be sick at the thought of how much pain she was in. "Guys please. I'm hanging on by a thread here. I don't want to be insensitive but you're leaking all over me and after Beth's pain I don't think I can take any more right now."

"I'm sorry Cara. We should have thought of that." Jonathan sat on the arm of the couch and brushed a hand over her hair. After a deep breath she continued.

"It was after the book and it got it. So we can assume that Christian now has it."

"Her hands," Thomas whispered.

"Her burns still hadn't healed and she was holding it so tight—" Cara grabbed her stomach, jumped up from the couch and ran outside. Jonathan followed her.

Thomas went to Beth's door and cracked it. She was laying on her side with her back to him. There was a fresh bandage on her covering the old wound and new bruising spread all over her back. She shifted and Thomas started to leave but was stopped by her voice.

"Cara?"

"It's Thomas, I'll get her."

"No, she's struggling right now. I just need some water." Her voice wasn't' right. She sounded like well, she sounded like someone had tried to choke the life out of her.

"I'll get it." Thomas kept his voice soft but inside anger burned through him. He took a few extra moments in the kitchen to get himself under control. Beth didn't need his anger.

"Thanks." Beth whispered as he handed her the glass. She was sitting up in bed but didn't rest her back even against the pillow. She tried to hold the glass but her newly bandaged hands made the task impossible.

"Here." Thomas held the glass to her mouth as she drank.

"Ouch." Beth touched her throat lightly with her wrapped hands. She looked down at them. "I look like a mummy." She smiled, then winced at her split lip.

"Take it easy. How can you even make a joke?"

"Really good pain killers."

"Ah." Thomas looked in her eyes and her slightly dazed expression confirmed it, she was high as a kite." "You're stoned."

"Yep. But nothing hurts so I'm good with that."

"I'll let you sleep."

"Wait. Tell Jonathan I'm sorry I lost the book." The anger bubbled up and Thomas was sure it was reflected on his face because Beth shrank back a little and that almost killed him right there.

"Forget the damn book. You almost died in there."

"Still here see." Beth waved her mummy hands at him. Thomas found his anger fleeing and being replaced by bewilderment. He shook his head.

"Was it Cavannah?"

"Cavannah!" Beth sort of screamed in a whisper. "That little bitch can't take me. She doesn't have that kind of power. I can't even believe you—"

"Okay, okay. Not Cavannah. Got it." Thomas laughed at Beth's outrage. He sobered and asked, "Do you know who or what it was?"

"Does it matter? It accomplished the goal of getting the book."

"It matters." Thomas turned to leave.

"Why?"

"I need to know so I can find it and kill it." Thomas shut the door quietly as he left.

CHAPTER 41

Beth took the day to recuperate, thankful for the healing herbs and the oh-so-wonderful pain medication. They'd argued all day about continuing with the invisibility spell but Beth won when she pointed out they needed to go on the offensive and get Christian now that he had the book and time was running out. They didn't think she was strong enough for all her injuries but she explained that her power didn't rely on the health of her body. Well, if she was mortally wounded maybe, but she didn't see the need to mention that. She still hurt everywhere, she knew her hands would scar and probably her back and her ego took a big hit, too. Jonathan had been almost as angry as Thomas when she apologized for losing the book. It was time to attack for once instead of being the target, and Beth was more than ready.

Beth cast her spell silently. She'd left out one small detail when they had gone over the plan and she hoped no one noticed.

"I can still see everyone," Mason said.

"You're supposed to be able to see each other," Beth replied dryly.

"How do we know it worked?"

"When the vampires don't kill you, you'll know." Beth smiled sweetly at him before turning away.

The sun was disappearing fast, and they needed to be outside. Being invisible wouldn't help them if the enemy saw the door opening by itself. They had gone out earlier and moved the cars. Saying good-bye to Beth, they melted into the woods.

Inside, Beth went to the bookshelf and pulled out one of the volumes. The next section of the shelves opened away from the wall. She ducked inside to wait, called Sheena in with her, and closed the shelf behind her. There was no need to make herself invisible. Taking a breath, she cast a deep sleeping spell on her wolf, then removed the shields from the house. They had been up for a long time, and she hadn't realized how vulnerable she would feel without them. This was the detail she had omitted. If Cavannah showed up again and the shields were in place, she would know Beth was still inside. Even if Cavannah didn't come, the vampires might know something of witches. They could get suspicious if they couldn't get in. She felt them coming, bowed her head, and prayed she made it so everyone could yell at her.

"Here they come," Thomas whispered to Jonathan from the trees.

They watched yet another van stop in Beth's drive. Jonathan found himself wondering how Christian kept convincing them that they would succeed. No one he sent had come back, or was this simply another distraction?

"They're going in," Mason commented.

"What do you mean they're going in?" Thomas' voice rose.

"I didn't even think about it, and of course she didn't mention it," said Cara. "She had to take the shields down to convince them she wasn't in there."

"We have to go back." Thomas rose from his crouch.

"No. I've got her. She's okay. I'll know if something is wrong. She's invisible, remember? Plus, she's got a hiding place. And she must have done something to quiet Sheena so she wouldn't go crazy with those things in the house."

"They're tearing the place apart." Jonathan could hear the damage being done inside Beth's house. If so much as a hair was damaged on Beth, there would be hell to pay when they caught up with those devils.

Minutes later the group exited the house. Jonathan took note that everyone was holding their breath. The vampires walked straight to the van and never even glanced in the direction of the trees. Seconds later, Beth appeared in a window and gave them the thumbs up sign to indicate that she was okay. Amused, Jonathan heard Thomas' sigh of relief.

They jumped into the waiting car. Rob didn't say a word to them. His lips were pressed into such a thin line Jonathan guessed Rob was struggling not to ask questions. He wondered what type of person performed such odd services "no questions asked". Rob had dark, close-cropped hair and if he wasn't mistaken, definitely some Irish in him. He followed the van. When it stopped, he let them out and drove off.

Beth had warned them that the spell would eventually wear off without her there to repeat it. It had originally been concocted to work with humans. Vampires' senses were much more acute and eventually they would "see" through it.

As their quarry entered the building, noise flowed from the open door. Jonathan led them around back.

"How many do you think are in there?" Mason withdrew both guns and checked his ammunition again.

"Six went in, but judging from the noise, I couldn't even begin to guess," Thomas answered. The warehouse had to be at least 6,000 square feet.

"There's a window up there," motioned Cara. "It doesn't look like it's completely blacked out. Let's take a peek. Christian may not even be in there." Cara headed towards a dumpster to boost herself up.

"You're not going to be tall enough to reach the window," said Jonathan. "Besides, I can tell you he's in there. I can sense him. There are also quite a few vampires, but I can't tell how many." Jonathan helped her up onto the dumpster, vaulted up himself, then lifted her onto his shoulders so she could see in the window.

"Shit!"

"What?" Jonathan shifted under her. He could have held her up forever, but he was impatient to see inside for himself.

Cara relayed what she saw, Christian in a white robe. He had several humans on their knees in supplication. It was feeding time, too. She counted ten humans. Probably thirty vampires. She wriggled down from Jonathan's shoulders and jumped off the dumpster. "I wish I had been wrong about that. I was hoping we wouldn't have to worry about anyone but Christian and his gang."

"Why don't we wait until sun up and smash the windows?" Mason turned to Jonathan.

"There's no guarantee they'll stay here until sunrise and the people not affected by the sunlight will probably protect the others. I think we'll all agree to minimize the harm to the humans." Jonathan looked around, and everyone nodded. "After they've had their fill, some of the vamps may leave. If we can lessen their numbers by even a few we'll have a chance."

"So we wait? Don't you think we should strike now before Beth's spell wears off?" Mason wanted to get going. "Besides that, if you can sense Christian being in there, what are the chances that he might sense you as well? We'll lose any chance for surprise."

"You have a point." Jonathan thought for a moment. If they went now, they could probably take out quite a few before they even realized what was going on.

"We go now."

CHAPTER 42

The front door of the building was closed. Cara stood, trying to determine how to get in without alerting anyone. Just when she was ready to push in fast, a straggler walked up and opened the door. It closed slowly as the four of them slid in behind, but no one seemed to notice. Christian didn't even glance their way; Beth's spell was still doing its thing.

The spell made them invisible, but they could still be heard so they relied on hand signals to move into position. Wanting to attack as many as they could at one time, Cara instructed the others to split up and pick the vamps in groups. Cara covered three vamps huddled in a corner in deep conversation. Two were basking in the afterglow of feeding, and Mason got them. Thomas stood behind four that were still feasting. Jonathan searched out Christian who was surrounded by the human followers who had already sated the group. Because his back was to the wall and he faced his mortal servants, Jonathan would have to go through them to get to him. Cara watched from across the room as Jonathan inched closer. Christian paused mid-sentence and looked around. Then his head whipped up. He blinked, then growled. The jig was up and all hell broke loose.

Cara aimed for the back of the head and hit all three marks. She turned and picked her next targets as Mason fired right into the center of his victims' hearts, and then moved on quickly. Thomas took care of two vamps by beheading. The other two in Thomas' group rose to attack, and Cara decided they made as a good a target as any. Confusion and mayhem set in as the vampires fell victim to an invisible killing force. They could hear gunshots and see their comrades drop; in one area heads went flying. But as of yet they could not see the source of their mysterious attackers. Wildly they began flailing out with their nails drawn, hoping to connect with whatever demons were besetting them. Meanwhile, Cara made her way towards Mason and Thomas, taking out or maiming whatever she could.

Eventually they stood in a small circle: two would cover the other while they reloaded. Thomas of course just kept swinging with every ounce of energy that he had. Apparently the spell was wearing off, because the vamps were becoming increasingly accurate in their counterattacks. Cara tried to see what was happening in Jonathan's corner; her attention drifted and a vamp slid too close, cracking her in the head. She cried out, and Thomas swung around, slicing the attacker with his long sword.

Cara lifted a hand to her eyebrow and came away with blood. *Greeat!* She wiped it as best she could but it kept seeping into her eye. Mason's gun jammed and he tossed it to the side; he had no time to play with it.

With Christian's growl, Jonathan had leapt over the misguided and slammed into him. He hit the wall, and Jonathan grabbed his robes, spinning and sending him back into the wall a few more times for good measure. Christian brought his claws up, slashing Jonathan across the face. Jonathan stumbled back, and Christian smiled, showing himself as he truly was. A few of the human followers shrieked at the sudden display of pure evil and ran. Jonathan watched them flee out the door.

"They were so easy, too. They practically begged me to take them. Valerie begged—"

Christian didn't quite finish as Jonathan grabbed him again, raised him over his head, and threw him to the ground. Christian rolled and tried to sweep Jonathan's feet but missed. Jonathan slipped a silver dagger from his sleeve, it sailed through the air, impaling itself in Christian's shoulder. He screamed, even as he rose he propelled himself toward Jonathan. Jonathan saw him coming and spun around, delivering a kick to Christian's midsection. He stumbled back, lowered himself, then sprang through the air at Jonathan, and they both tumbled. Jonathan came up on top, slipping a second dagger from his sleeve and stabbing Christian in the heart. Christian gasped and screamed. Jonathan pinned Christian's wrists so that he couldn't remove the blade. Christian bucked and writhed but couldn't dislodge him.

"Thomas!" Jonathan was managing to hold Christian down, but he didn't know how much longer he could last.

"Can't get away right now!"

Jonathan looked over. Thomas and the others had cut the number considerably. Only eight were left circling them, but the spell was totally gone now and every move Thomas made towards Jonathan was cut off by at least three vamps. Mason and Cara tried to shift the circle they had made, trying to give Thomas the opening he would need to slip out and help Jonathan.

Jonathan had almost decided to finish Christian himself when a particularly devoted human follower jumped on his back. The woman clawed at Jonathan and beat at him. He tried to ignore the punishment, but he found his grip on Christian weakening. Suddenly one of Christian's hands slipped free; jerking the dagger from his own chest, he spun it and sank it into Jonathan's. Still gasping, he weakly dragged himself from underneath Jonathan as he fell back, pinning the screaming woman under him. Jonathan wrapped his fingers around the knife shaft and pulled it from his body. Blood spilled freely. Jonathan knew it hadn't pierced the heart, but it sure hurt like a bitch.

Cara looked to Jonathan just as Christian sank the knife in him. Banking all her emotion she pulled her arm from the vampire that was trying to wrest her gun from her and shot him in the face. Breaking from the circle, she dropped her empty clips and put new ones in en route to Christian. He was still recovering on the floor with his rescuer leaning over him, wailing. He looked up at Cara approaching.

"Get her my sister, she'll kill me!"

The woman went after Cara who broke into a run, went low, and just as the woman jumped her she raised up and elbowed her in the face. Blood spurted from her nose and she went down. Cara continued, and as she reached Christian he rose to his feet. She fired once, aiming for his heart. He turned at the last moment and the shot hit him in the shoulder. *Damn these vampires are fast!* He came at her. Before she knew it her weapons were gone and he had her by the throat. Cara had forgotten that Christian had perfected the power Jonathan had. The younger ones she had been battling didn't have his speed.

Dangling from Christian's hand, she could see that Thomas and Mason had finished off the remaining vamps. They moved beside Jonathan who had recovered enough to stumble towards where his friends had been fighting. The three of them stood fifteen feet away, but it might as well have been a mile.

"Somebody fucking kill him!" Cara screamed. Christian tightened his hold, cutting off her air. She clawed at his hand but it didn't affect him.

"Once again I hold someone dear to you," Christian yelled to Jonathan. He pulled Cara's struggling body toward him and licked the blood off her face. "Mmm, yummy."

"You kill her, and you know you're dead." Jonathan's voice was like ice.

"Perhaps, but she will still be gone." Christian loosed his hold on Cara enough for her to be able to draw air in. After a couple of breaths, she felt herself go limp.

"The excitement must have been too much for her. Now tell your new friends to drop their weapons, and maybe I won't snap her neck."

"Thomas. Mason."

She heard their weapons fall to the floor.

"Good. Good. Now, Thomas, I've changed my mind, you may pick up your long sword." Thomas must have hesitated because Christian demanded, "Now!" followed by "Good boy. I have a favor, Thomas. I'd do it myself, but as you can see I'm rather busy. If you would be so kind as to sever Jonathan's head."

Cara could feel his grin shimmer up his arm and into her.

"Come now. We haven't all night."

"No." She heard the sword thrown down.

"It's him or it's her." Christian gave Cara's limp body a shake. "Let's ask Jonathan which he would prefer."

"Do it, Thomas," Jonathan whispered hoarsely.

"No." Thomas commanded.

"Pick up the sword, Thomas. It's my life. Do it!"

"It's her life, too, and I know what she would say."

"What would she say, Thomas?" Christian asked.

"She would say—"

"Go fuck yourself!" Cara's head popped up, startling Christian. She kicked him with every ounce of power she could muster right between the legs, and they both hit the floor. Everyone scrambled for weapons. Cara crawled to the side, and Jonathan nearly flew to pull her from Christian's reach. In response, Christian used his speed to rush Thomas and Mason. Mason got a shot off before Christian picked him up and threw him. Thomas swung at him with the short sword, but missed as Christian saw the flash of metal and ducked just in time. He headed straight for the open door. Jonathan was not two yards behind. Thomas made sure Mason was still breathing, then checked Cara who was watching Christian flee with Jonathan in pursuit.

"That was some kick!" Thomas knelt beside her.

"Works every time." Cara touched her head gingerly. "Stitches?"

"Maybe a couple." Thomas helped Cara over to where Mason was.

"I guess we wait," Cara said as she began checking over Mason.

Half an hour later, Jonathan returned; he hadn't caught Christian, though he had come close enough to draw blood once again with his elongated nails. Mason was still unconscious. Jonathan ran a finger along the bruising on Cara's neck. Concerned, he took in the double set of fang marks on her skin.

"I hate seeing you hurt."

"That's sweet honey but how are we getting home?"

CHAPTER 43

Beth poured antiseptic on a cotton ball.

"Ouch! Damn! That hurts worse than when I got hit."

"That means it's healing," Beth sniffed.

"No, that means you're killing me." Cara eyed Beth warily as she came at her with another cotton ball. "Is this payback for when I nursed you, cause I was only trying to help. Jonathan tell her to be nice to me."

"I'm not getting anywhere near this conversation."

"Smart Man. Now quit being a baby." Beth finished cleaning and applied four butterfly stitches. "I'm glad that Mason thought to bring some supplies back yesterday when you two were out."

"If this keeps going much longer, we're going to have a doctor move into your house."

They both jumped when the phone rang.

"I don't want to answer it," Beth said even as she picked it up. She didn't say much and wasn't on long before she hung up.

"Mason has a slight concussion; they're on the way here now."

"Now that I know he's okay I'm stealing the guest room." Cara headed toward the room and grabbed Jonathan's hand.

"So miss fearless cop is afraid of cotton balls." Jonathan smiled down at her.

"Do you want to sleep alone?" Cara asked.

"No, um *honey,* I don't."

"Then never mention the cotton balls again. I didn't think you caught that." Cara mumbled as they entered the room.

"Yes, *honey,* I caught it."

"Oh, lord." Cara shut the door.

Beth waited for Thomas and Mason to return. Mason walked in and headed straight for the bedroom. Thomas joined Beth in the kitchen, where she was still trying to clean.

"Why do I have the feeling I'm sleeping on the couch?"

"It opens into a bed."

"Oh fun."

"Beggars can't be choosers."

"True. How's Cara?"

"Sleeping. I patched her up and sent her to bed." Beth finished wiping off the counter. She didn't really have anything to say to Thomas, but she sensed he was hurting.

"About earlier, Beth—"

"I don't have the energy to argue with you about it anymore. I don't really like the way you went about trying to get information out of me." She threw the towel into the sink.

"That's one of the things I wanted to talk to you about. I shouldn't have pushed you, especially since I said I wouldn't. It sort of slipped out. I can't help wondering about it, but I won't mention it again."

"Fine." She wasn't sure if she believed him or not. "What else?"

"The shields. You didn't happen to mention that there would be none on the house."

"Must have slipped my mind. I am alive and well, so I don't see that there's anything to talk about."

"You keep putting yourself in danger, Beth."

"And where were you last night?"

"That's different."

"How so?" Beth's foot tapped the floor. She was waiting for chauvinistic stupidity to come out of Thomas' mouth.

"Did you find something in the pages you have left of the book?"

Beth enjoyed Thomas' neat change of subject and felt herself smiling. "Only one thing of interest. It seems that Christian can change someone twice a year."

"It's been three hundred years since Jonathan last saw him. That's— that's six hundred he could have turned since then."

"Not quite," she replied. "Cara was right. He would have to be sure it was the type of person that would be willing to kill for the fun of it. After all, he doesn't want another Jonathan."

"I'm sure he could find six hundred psychos in three hundred years."

"Maybe, but he also wants them to take orders from him. The ones he sent here were vicious, but they also followed in the footsteps of others who had failed. You'd have to find a certain kind of person. Someone smart enough not to give away the entire plan, dumb enough to follow orders blindly, and nasty enough to murder for the hell of it. Besides, if he had that many, they would have just swooped in here and taken us all out."

"True," he relented.

"As far as his minions turning others, they would have to reach maturity. That takes about two hundred and fifty years. That's why the ones who came here weren't as fast as Jonathan or as strong. They're too young, or maybe Christian isn't sharing information. He wants to dominate."

"Anything about what will happen to Jonathan if he kills Christian?" asked Thomas.

"Couple of comments. One, everything the guilty party holds dear will be destroyed. Two, the world as he knows it will unravel. Basically the same thing just put a different way."

"Everything he holds dear. Does that mean the people he holds dear?"

"I don't know. I didn't think of it that way. If that's what it means, you and Cara are toast if he kills Christian."

"Cara's toast," Thomas corrected.

"Oh no. I told you, the older versions were incredibly powerful. You would go too, Boy Wonder."

"I don't think I like that. And you're taking Cara's demise awfully well."

"I honestly don't think that's it. The ones who set up these rules were guardians. It doesn't seem in their nature to take an innocent life."

"How much further do you have to go?"

"There's text in there I'm not familiar with. I contacted my governors and they're sending me something that may help." Beth moved into the living room and sat on the couch.

"Did you go into a trance and conjure them up?"

"No, I used the phone." Beth didn't care for the humor. She didn't know how to take it from him.

"Relax, I'm just joking." Thomas took the seat across from her. "Explain the governors to me."

"Why?"

"I'm curious."

"In the simplest terms they're like the supreme court of witches, except there are thirteen."

"What do they do?"

"Uphold our laws. If a witch isn't brought to justice through normal means, they step in."

"How are they chosen?"

"The retiree chooses a successor, and they are voted in by the rest. It seems to work well."

"They must lead boring lives. How many true witches can there be?"

"At last count there were three million, full-blooded witches. But that's not all they do. They are responsible for dealing with dark witches. Not to mention handling the relationships with other species. Boring, their lives are not."

"Three million! I had no idea."

"They don't all live in Florida," she smiled.

"Are they all like you? I mean, you seem to have a fair amount of talent."

"Some more, some less. Some can only perform certain types of magic. Just like any human, our talents lay in different areas."

"Where do yours lay?"

"Are you writing a story or something? I feel like I'm being interviewed."

"I just want to know more." Thomas laughed. "If you want, I'll give it a rest and turn in."

Beth sat for moment after Thomas left and thought of all the sleep they had missed. Even when they had a respite, they did it on pins and needles. Maybe she could help them to get some real rest.

CHAPTER 44

Thomas woke up the next morning feeling rested and relaxed. He couldn't remember ever having slept that well. He glanced at the clock. *Ten o'clock!* He sprang out of bed. He never got up that late. Grabbing clothes, he headed to the shower in his pajama bottoms. Mason was just coming out.

"How's the head?" Thomas asked as they passed in the hall.

"Fine. Great actually. I slept better than I ever have." Mason walked toward the smell of coffee.

Thomas quickly shaved and showered. When he joined everyone in the kitchen they were discussing what the next move would be. Jonathan was out for the day but there had to be something they could do. Thomas poured his coffee and listened to Cara's idea of following Vinton. She paused to take a bite of a bacon sandwich.

"I'm starving. I slept so well last night and woke up ravenous; we did skip dinner last night," Cara said after she swallowed her food.

Thomas caught Beth smiling as she lifted her Diet Coke to her lips.

"What?" He had this sinking feeling in his stomach.

"Nothing," Beth said, her eyes going wide.

"Not nothing, something. You're grinning like you know something that no one else does. What did you do?" Thomas snapped at her. Beth's grin vanished.

"What do you mean?" she asked cautiously.

"Everybody slept like babies. What did you do?"

"No one has gotten any real rest, so I just did a little something to make sure everyone got the sleep they needed. Healing sleep. I didn't have anything to do with what time you got up. Your body slumbered until it got what it needed." Beth looked at Thomas uncertainly.

187

"Works for me," Mason said.

Thomas felt Cara watching him as he stared at Beth. "Well, it doesn't work for me. Keep your spells to yourself. No wonder you don't leave, you're a danger to society." As soon as the words left his mouth he wanted to pull them back. *God, what an idiot I am!* He expected her to tear up as she'd done the first time he'd hurt her. He didn't expect her Coke can to come flying at him. He ducked just in time and saw a smile hovering on Cara's lips. Beth's temper worked on slow burn, but once it heated up it was like a four-alarm fire.

"Fine, you jerk. The next time you need to be invisible so your ass doesn't get creamed, I guess you'll be out of luck, won't you?" Beth turned, picked up a salt shaker, and winged that at him, too.

Mason grabbed his plate and left the kitchen. Cara went with him, covering her mouth with her hand.

"And the next time someone comes here to slay us, you can wait outside the house so my shields don't bother you!"

Thomas managed to dodge the salt shaker. When she stopped to look around for another projectile, he moved in and grabbed her wrists. He pressed her back against the refrigerator, pinning her arms between them.

"I'm sorry!" He could still see danger in her eyes. "It just took me by surprise. I'm sorry, I overreacted." Beth took a couple of breaths and he felt her temper coming back under control. Thomas slowly released her and stepped back. "Everything fine now?" he asked as he backed away from her.

"Just give me a minute."

"Alright." Thomas turned and walked away. A bottle of Tylenol smacked him in the back of the head.

"Now I'm fine," Beth said as she walked past him.

Thomas entered the dining room rubbing the back of his head. Mason was laughing, looking down at his plate. "Shut up," Thomas scowled at him.

"We should still be looking for Christian. Take him out." Mason said.

"That worked well last night, and we had Jonathan with us." Thomas pointed out.

"We also had thirty or so other vamps to contend with, and a few wild-eyed humans. Let's plan a little better and make sure we have the upper hand. Besides, the thing that tipped Christian off was sensing Jonathan's presence with us. No offense to him, but there might be some advantages in not having him with us. Plus it's daytime, it's about time we hunted them while they were at their weakest."

"True," Thomas lowered his head into his hands. "What were you saying earlier about following Vinton?"

"We could, but we'd have to wait until he gets out of the hospital." Cara glanced towards Mason.

"Was that only yesterday?"

"Yep." Mason got up from the table and took his plate to the kitchen.

"So where does all this leave us?" Thomas asked.

"Nowhere," Mason answered as he came back into the room. "But I can't sit here all day and wait for Christian to knock on the door. I don't think any of my snitches know I'm suspended. I'll make the rounds again."

"I'll go back through the missing person files," added Cara. "See if I recognize any of them. Maybe they returned after last night. They might be able to tell us if Christian has a second home." Cara pushed away from the table to retrieve the files.

"I'll go back to my book." Beth headed for the library.

"Well, what the hell do I do?" Thomas asked quietly.

"You can come with me," Mason said from behind him.

"Why not?" Thomas got up and followed him out the door.

There was no conversation as they pulled away from Beth's. They hit a few spots where Mason's connections usually hung out but turned up nothing. They had just pulled into Erin's Bar when Mason's phone rang. Cara had discovered that a young woman had recently been reported missing and then found late last night. Could be a lead. She gave Mason the information he would need to find her. He hesitated; he shouldn't really take Thomas with him, but then again he probably shouldn't be going himself.

"On our way," Mason told Cara before hanging up and telling Thomas the turn of events as they pulled from the parking lot.

The modest home was relatively close, and they pulled up in front in mere minutes. When they knocked on the door, it was opened by a woman who reminded Mason of Betty White.

"Can I help you?" She looked tired, but she smiled at them.

"Yes, ma'am, we're with the Miami police department." He didn't get any further before the woman stopped him.

"I called this morning and told them she had come home. I explained that everything was okay." She seemed a little flustered.

"Yes, ma'am, but we'd still like to talk to Miss Cain." Mason put his best civil servant smile on. Thomas just tried to look harmless.

"Betty" looked from one to the other, then moved aside for them to come in. "I'm Mrs. Cain, Michelle's mother. Course you probably already figured that out. She came home late last night. It was awful. She was a mess. She only let me call the police to say she was home. I may look a little naïve, but I know something was done to her. Maybe you can convince her to talk. She just sat in my arms and cried for hours." Mrs. Cain spoke quietly as she showed them into the living room and gave them a seat. "If someone hurt her in some way—" she stopped and took a deep breath. "I want you to put them in a cage and keep them there. She's not the same as when she left, and I just don't know what to do. I'll go get Michelle."

Thomas looked at Mason wondering just how different Michelle was. When the thin girl walked into the room, she didn't shrink from the light pouring in the windows. But the turtleneck she wore told them this was the girl. For that Thomas sent up a silent thanks to God.

She was pale and drawn. She was a pretty girl with soft features, but now she seemed to crumble into herself. Michelle looked from Mason to Thomas and took a seat across from them.

"I'll go make some tea." Mrs. Cain seemed wise enough to understand that sometimes there were things daughters didn't want their mothers to know.

"I didn't do anything wrong," her voice shook.

"I know, Michelle. May I call you that?" Michelle gave Mason a week nod. "Thank you. We just want to ask a few questions about your disappearance. Okay?"

"I didn't do anything wrong," she said again.

"No, you didn't, Michelle," Mason's voice was soft and soothing. "Someone did though, didn't they?"

"Yes," she whispered.

"Can you tell us about it?"

"I—I thought it was a church. I met this guy at school. He said he wanted to introduce me to God. We used to go a lot, to church I mean, but we moved and haven't found a new one. So, I went and . . . it, it was horrible. I don't know what he was, but I know he wasn't God." She was crying now. "They wouldn't let me leave. I was so afraid they were going to rape me, but there were other women who were willing so they left me alone for that, but they—they—" Michelle's sobs were coming faster now, she had to force the words out, "They fed on my neck, and somehow I think it was worse."

"Take a couple breaths, Michelle. You're okay now. Did you only stay at one location?"

Thomas hated seeing Mason push her after what she had been through, but he accepted that others might suffer if he didn't.

"There was a place in the everglades. They didn't care if I saw where they were going. I don't think they intended to let me go." Michelle leaned back against the chair and closed her eyes.

"Can you show me this place on a map?" Mason's pulse rate went up.

"Probably," she whispered. "He's going to come for me, you know."

"Why didn't you want your mother to call the police last night?"

"I didn't think they could protect me."

"So why tell me now?"

"Because I saw you last night. You know how to deal with those creatures. Are you really police?"

"I am." Mason glanced at Thomas.

Tea was served and a map brought out. They left assuring Michelle she would have protection.

"I don't have any authority to put anyone on her. Can you place one of your guys over here?" Mason asked as they got in the car.

"I spoke to Mrs. Cain while Michelle gave you the location. I'm having some men pick them up in an hour. They'll be taken to a safe house until this is over."

Mason pulled out his cell to call Beth. He gave her a run down on the situation and told her they were headed to the second site. Thomas could hear her berating him, but she relented when he reminded her that they intended to plan better this time. There would be no rushing in.

CHAPTER 45

osquitoes buzzed around Mason as he left the car and scanned the area. This time of year they swarmed everywhere, but they were particularly bad in the swamp. The everglades were growing more popular every year. You could visit Indian reservations, take an air boat ride, or do any number of things, but this stretch of road was off the beaten track. The place they were looking for was barely visible in the distance. Mason went to the trunk and pulled out binoculars. Zooming in, he couldn't detect any activity, but that didn't mean there wasn't anything happening on the inside.

"See anything?" Thomas asked over the hood of the car.

"Not a damn thing. I can't see anything except the roof." Mason passed the binoculars to give Thomas a look.

"Well, that's promising. What do you want to do?"

"Let's walk around, see if we can get a better look. There's not a cloud in the sky. As long as we don't go in, he can't come out." Mason locked the car and checked his weapons. He was going to have to apologize to Beth. When he'd first seen the number of silver bullets she had ordered, he'd thought she had gone overboard. Now he felt he should fall on his knees and thank her.

Leaving the car and crossing the road, Mason led Thomas down off the built-up roadway so they weren't so visible. But there was no path and the going was slow. By the time they were halfway, their shirts stuck to their backs and sweat dripped down their faces.

"Florida humidity, ain't it grand!" Mason pulled his shirt away from his skin. Thomas grunted. They reached the edge of the wood around the house. Surveying the structure, Mason noticed the blackened windows. He motioned to Thomas and pointed. They were

193

in the right place. Circling the building they looked for a way to get closer without losing cover. Creeping along the back they saw that the woods abutted the back wall of the building. Shrubbery blocked the bottom windows. Mason noted that whoever had painted the windows had done a poor job here, thinking the shrubs would block anything they missed. Leaning down, Mason shifted the shrubs to the side. The place was empty. The only area he couldn't see into was some type of loft. "What do you think?"

"I don't know. I couldn't see up into that loft area." Thomas wiped the sweat from his forehead.

"It's broad daylight. I say we smash the windows, open the doors, and go in. He won't be able to come at us if we stay in the light."

"Is that your way of planning better?" Thomas grinned at him.

"Well, we could wait till dark."

"Not funny." Thomas looked at the building and back at Mason. "I don't have a sword."

"Fill him with enough silver, and we can drag him into the sun."

"You just want to break something." Thomas moved toward the building.

"Yeah, there is that."

Picking up large pieces of wood they began systematically breaking the windows, then clearing away the glass so that the optimum amount of sunlight could shine in. The ones they couldn't reach they threw rocks into. Nothing stirred. Moving to the front they arrived at a pair of large double doors. Mason handed Thomas a gun, then pulled out two of his own.

"How many of these do you have?"

"Enough, I hope."

Thomas took his free hand and opened the doors. They stood in the doorway and Mason heard movement. Looking up to the loft, a figure appeared in the entrance, a huge figure.

"That's not Christian," Mason said.

"I don't know what that is."

The creature dropped easily from the loft to the floor. It didn't seem in any hurry, stopping when it hit the ground. Mason stood ready to fire two handed. Then he handed his second gun to Thomas and took out his phone.

"You're making a call?" Thomas said in a low voice.

Mason ignored him and dialed. "Okay, what's seven feet tall, human shape, gray, wrinkly, and has pointy ears?" Mason asked.

"Huh?" Beth sounded startled by the question. "Mason, is this some kind of game?"

"Baby, I wish. It's standing about two hundred feet away."

"Oh, shit! Okay, okay, seven feet, gray. Gremlin, it's a gremlin!"

"Can I kill it?" Mason lowered his voice even more as the gremlin took a few steps forward.

"Yeah, do you have a bazooka? Leave, get out of there now!"

"The silver bullets won't work?"

"What you're firing with won't pierce its skin. Quit talking and move!" Beth was getting more agitated.

"Calm down. It's not moving toward us. It's just kind of watching."

"Christian is probably asleep. He needed to heal from last night. Cara said the dagger went into his heart. Silver wounds heal slowly. He's not coming at you because he hasn't been told to yet. If Christian wakes and orders him to attack he will, or if you try to get near Christian he'll go for you. They're like nether world mercenaries. Are you leaving yet?"

"If he's here, Christian's here. It's broad daylight; we'll never get a better chance. Think, Beth, is there any way past this thing?" Mason could practically hear her brain ticking.

"It's a long shot. The only soft spot they have is on the inner thigh. If you can get him there he wouldn't be able to walk. Then if you can make it past the long reach—I'm sure you've noticed the length of his arms—take out his eyes. You *might* be able to get past him then."

"Thanks, I'll call you back." Mason clicked her off as she was still screaming at him to leave.

"Well?"

"Gremlin."

"I thought Hollywood made those up. I also thought they were about two feet tall.

"Their only soft spot is on the inner thigh. Take out the legs, and he can't get around. Then go for the eyes." The gremlin came forward a few more feet. "Your call."

"I say we go for it. We'll split up, come at it from both sides."

"If we miss, run like hell. Beth made it sound like he wouldn't stray too far from Christian."

"Got it. By the way, what's with this 'Baby'?"

"What?"

"You called Beth 'Baby.' "

"So?"

"Something going on there?"

"No. I do occasionally do something chauvinistic. I don't do it to Cara 'cause she'd hurt me."

"Okay. Let's move."

Going through the doorway they went in opposite directions. The gremlin glanced between them, then focused on Mason. Mason took the side that led to the loft, and turned toward him. Mason fired and missed his target. He fired again and missed. Thomas shot at its back, hoping to distract it to give Mason a better chance, but the gremlin didn't turn. The bullets hit, seemed to stick to the gray skin for a moment, then fall to the ground.

The gremlin took its time advancing on Mason, as though he knew the weapons couldn't hurt him. Mason fired and hit right above the knee. The gremlin's leg buckled for a split second and his leg twisted, exposing his inner thigh. Mason fired twice, striking his target dead center both times. The gremlin dropped to the ground, howling like nothing either of them had ever heard before. Mason tried to get closer, but it swung its arms out. Thomas moved in, distracting it. Mason stalked closer, but the gremlin's arms were swinging wildly now, pain and fury mingling. One clawed hand connected, knocking the gun from Mason's left hand. A roar of fury filled the air, this time from another source, not the wounded beast in front of them. Mason looked up at the loft. Christian stood just outside of the light.

"Get up! Get up and kill them!"

Mason turned quickly to retrieve his gun and picked it up from the floor while Thomas was focused on Christian. Taking a step forward and aiming at the vampire, Thomas mustn't have realized he'd put himself in the path of the gremlin's flailing arms. It grabbed his leg and pulled him down.

Mason ran at them, firing as he went. Not releasing the hold on Thomas, it lashed out at Mason with its other hand. Pain seared his left arm. The gremlin turned back to his struggling captive. Mason immediately jumped on its back, hoping to get at one of its eyes. One incredibly long arm reached back, grabbed him, and flung him away. He hit and slid across the concrete floor. Jumping to his feet, he ran back.

The gremlin made it to its feet, dragging Thomas with it. Tossing him into the air like a doll, the gremlin caught Thomas by the head and gave him a vicious twist, breaking his neck. Mason stopped in mid stride. Horrified, he watched the gremlin throw Thomas' body to the side and advance toward him. It was limping badly, but it was also protecting its weak spot. Mason fired anyway. After three shots the gun clicked empty. He looked at it in disbelief, then in slow motion stared at Christian's silhouette and the gremlin making its way slowly toward him. Gritting his teeth he shoved his gun in his holster and dove toward the gun Thomas had dropped. Scooping it up, he fired toward Christian and the gremlin. Christian faded into the darkness. The gremlin kept coming. When the bullets were gone, frustration welled up, choking him. He hated it, but he only had one option left.

Run.

He didn't stop until he reached the car. He got in and rested his head on the back of the seat. His arms stung and throbbed, especially his left one. Looking down he saw that blood had already soaked through his shirt and was running down his arm.

Dead. Thomas was dead.

Supposedly he could come back. Hopefully he would. But Mason knew he would never be able to rid himself of the vision of that thing snapping Thomas' neck. To him, dead was dead.

Mason had that same sick feeling he'd gotten when his fellow cops had been killed. He kept telling himself Thomas wasn't dead, but he didn't believe his own voice.

CHAPTER 46

Mason drove as long as he could. The throbbing in his arm built until he felt it throughout his body. Pulling off to the side of the road, he phoned Cara.

"I can't drive anymore. You have to come get me." Mason gave her his location and clicked off.

Cara stared at the phone for a second before moving into high gear. She told Beth where she was going and promised to call when she reached them. Thomas must be in bad shape if he couldn't drive either. She looked at the sky as she drove and wondered what could have happened to them in broad daylight. Beth had said Mason asked about gremlins. They sounded like nasty creatures.

Twenty minutes later, Cara pulled up behind Mason's car. She could see his head lolling to the side. Jumping out, she ran and pulled the door open. Mason weakly tried to hold up his gun, but the blood loss had depleted his strength. Cara helped him into her car and drove him straight to the hospital. She didn't need to ask any questions. If Thomas had been alive, she knew Mason wouldn't have left him. Her heart did a slow roll in her chest. She'd known him for a short time, but he'd been the type of person to stand at your back and guard it with his life. That didn't happen every day. Mason was too out of it to answer the hows and whys.

The emergency room took him right away and she used the time in the waiting room to phone Beth.

"Sorry I didn't call you right away. Mason's arm looks like something was chewing on it. He's lost a lot of blood."

"How's Thomas?"

"He didn't make it." Cara's voice was soft.

"No! Oh no!" A pause on the line. "He'll come back though. They said he could come back."

"I hope he can. Are you okay?"

"Yes. No. No, I'm not, Cara. Gremlins are never easy; he must have suffered." Cara could hear her soft sobs. "Jonathan's still out, should I wake him?"

"No. I'll call you later. In the meantime, you keep yourself safe, you hear?"

Cara said good-bye and leaned her head against the wall. "Oh, Thomas. Come back soon," she whispered.

Three hours later she was allowed into the emergency unit with Mason.

"Hey. You look better."

"That's funny, I feel like shit. He's gone, Cara."

"I know."

"How do you know?"

"Because I know you, Mason. If there had been a breath in his body, you would have brought him back with you."

"Yeah, I'm a regular prince. I got him killed."

"What?"

"I wanted to go in. I wanted Christian dead. All I could see was the closet in my apartment. I felt like those four officers were looking down from that shelf, screaming for justice. I knew it was a huge risk, and I talked Thomas into going in anyway."

"Thomas has lived in this world a long time. He knew the danger."

"I'll try to remember that every time I close my eyes and see that thing snap his neck like a twig."

Cara said nothing else. She sat by his bedside while he dozed. At six o'clock Mason awoke with a start.

"What time is it?"

"Six."

"Let's go." Mason sat up.

"Mason, you lost a lot of blood. You need to rest."

"Sure, I'll just kick back and relax while you play hero."

"You have twenty stitches in your arm. You belong here."

"No. If they come for me here, somebody may get in the way." Mason ignored the rest of her arguments and detached himself from the hospital bed. He looked around for his shirt and pants and then glanced at Cara.

"I'll walk out of here just like this. Where are my clothes?"

"You're not going anywhere."

A sturdy-looking nurse walked into the room. "What did you do?" She rounded the side of the bed and saw the IV lying on the floor.

"I'm leaving. Where are my clothes?" Mason asked pleasantly.

"I'm getting the doctor." The nurse fled the room.

When the doctor arrived, no amount of threats and warnings could sway Mason. Eventually he was wheeled out of the hospital in only his jeans. His shirt had been cut off in the emergency room.

"You are such a man!" Cara slammed the driver's side door.

"Thanks."

"That wasn't a compliment."

When they arrived at Beth's, Cara watched as Mason took one look at her swollen, red eyes and hugged her with his good arm for a moment, planting a kiss on the top of her head. Jonathan stood in the doorway just out of reach of the last of the sun.

Beth closed the door. "Thomas will be back, right?"

"Yes, but it's hard for him. He doesn't like taking over a body, even if they no longer have any use for it. It took him six months to come back last time." Jonathan was silent a moment. "Please tell me what happened."

Mason reported the tale to Jonathan as if he were making a police report. Facts, details, but he ended with, "It was my fault. I got him killed."

Jonathan gave a halfhearted laugh. "I don't think so. You couldn't have gotten Thomas in that building with a team of wild horses if he hadn't wanted to go."

"If he knew I would have gone without him, would he have gone in then?"

Jonathan didn't answer.

"That's what I thought." Mason's eyes flickered with exhaustion. Cara and Beth took him to the bedroom and Beth sat beside him. She looked over the doctor's handiwork, then watched with concern the exhaustion evidenced in Mason's face.

"Trust me?" Beth asked softly as she ran a hand over his forehead.

"Yes," Mason said without hesitation. Beth smiled down at him.

"Close your eyes." Mason obeyed and Beth let both of her hands hover a few inches above his body. She started at his head and worked her way down, humming a little tune as she went. When she finished she left the room quietly and walked to the dining room. Cara sat at the table.

"He'll sleep for a little while now," Beth said as she took the seat beside Cara.

"What did you do?"

"Sleep can be healing, everybody knows that, but there's a certain, well, place in sleep that's more conducive. It's not just his body that needs it. His mind can use the break, too. I put him somewhere that he can relax, his body can mend faster and rejuvenate itself. I also pushed my own energy in. It'll speed up the healing and help him regain his equilibrium."

"So you're a healer now, too?"

"Almost any witch can do that. Power or energy can be taken from anyone, so long as they give it willingly."

"Can you bring someone back from the dead?"

"I can only speed along recovery. If it's too severe or traumatic, I can't do anything." Sitting at Beth's table Cara fell quiet. There was nothing to do anymore. They had no leads as to where Christian might flee. Thomas was dead, at least for now. Mason was too badly injured to go looking for more trouble. All they could do was wait. Eventually Christian would come for them. They still had the Elder ring. Death would knock on the door.

CHAPTER 47

Mason slept for the rest of the evening and into the next afternoon. Sheena didn't leave his side. There had been no activity during the night. Beth worked on translating Jonathan's book, but without the help the governors were sending she couldn't get far. Cara managed to sleep. She felt good when she woke up and wondered if Beth had "gotten" her as well. A thought occurred to her as she took a shower that morning. *All the energy that Beth was giving away, was it having any affect on her? Could Beth simply "recharge," or did it have an ill consequence?*

When she left the shower, Beth had already gone to sleep. They had taken shifts during the night, and Cara decided to let her rest.

Cara spent the afternoon combing over reports for the umpteenth time. She was almost positive there was nothing in them that she hadn't already seen and thought of. When she'd had enough, she flipped through the newspaper. Gee, no difference from her police reports. More chaos.

"You look happy," Mason ventured as he walked into the dining room. Other than the bandages he didn't look any worse for wear. Sheena padded along beside him.

"Looks like you've made a friend," Cara nodded toward the wolf.

"Maybe she's waiting for me to drop dead so she can dance on my grave." Mason eyed the animal. The wolf eyed him back, made a low growling noise, and headed off to the library.

"Looks like you just lost a friend," Cara laughed.

Beth came in stretching, flipped on the television and closed the heavy drapes, probably in case Jonathan rose early. They stared as a news report of a man found dead in an abandoned barn out in the everglades flashed on the screen. Thomas' driver's license picture popped on the screen. Anyone with any information was directed to contact the police. Beth turned the television off.

"Is there anything at the scene that could come back at you, Mason?" Cara set her plate in the dishwasher.

"No." Mason still stared at the blank screen. "I don't know what to do now."

"We wait for Christian to come to us. That's all we can do." Cara took Mason's hand and led him into the living room.

"Will we win?" Mason collapsed in a chair.

"I don't know. How badly did you wound the gremlin?"

"His right leg is pretty much shot, but I don't know how fast they heal."

"Slowly," Beth said coming into the room.

"How slowly?"

"To heal he'll have to hibernate."

"You can explain that another time," Mason grumbled.

Sheena paced back and forth in front of the door.

"Does she need to go out?" Mason asked as he eyed the wolf.

"No. Someone's coming."

Guns and swords appeared seemingly out of thin air.

"I don't think they mean any harm, but I can't be sure." Beth looked at Sheena. Sheena whined.

"Your dog doesn't know either," Mason mocked. Sheena bared her teeth at him.

"You call her a dog again and you'll see how bad tempered she is." Beth looked to the front. "I'll get the door."

"No, I'll get it." Mason moved around Sheena and looked out the peephole. "I don't see anything."

"I'm sure there's someone there," Beth shrugged.

Mason yanked open the door and then slammed it shut as quickly, pressing his back against it.

"What? What is it?" Cara asked. She had visions of bodies being dropped on the doorstep.

"I don't know." Mason looked at Beth. "They're green. And little."

"Oh, shit!" Beth's hands covered her mouth.

"What are they?" Mason took his other gun out.

"Open the door, Mason. They are the help the governors sent, and don't call them green." Beth pushed him out of the way and opened the door. By the time she ushered the confused Treshcans inside, the weapons had disappeared.

A man and a woman entered and looked around. Cara watched as they zeroed in on Jonathan and started toward him. They talked excitedly to one another in high singsong voices.

Green wasn't the precise shade of their skin. It was closer to aquamarine, and they seemed to shimmer. Both were slim and attractive, with eyes that seemed to be clear but for a glimmer of color that reflected from their skin.

Approaching Jonathan, they made it just above his kneecaps.

"Never seen one this close," the man said, pulling a chair from the dining room and moving it right in front of Jonathan. He climbed up and still only made it to Jonathan's chest. He peered into Jonathan's face as Cara looked on, a smile spreading across her lips.

"Dear, perhaps we should introduce ourselves before you begin. I do apologize; sometimes Rory's studies overtake his manners." The woman's smile lit up her face. "This is my husband, Rory, and I'm Grettel Premidian. We're here to help you translate a tome."

"Sorry, I get carried away sometimes." He offered his hand to Jonathan. Jonathan took it gingerly.

"Don't be afraid, old man, you can't hurt me," Rory grinned. Cara enjoyed Jonathan's indulgent smile. Rory's eyes narrowed and removing his hand from Jonathan's, he took a deep breath and shoved both of his tiny fists into Jonathan's chest. Jonathan lifted off the ground and landed on his backside. "There, now we all know where we stand." Rory looked at Mason, whose gun was drawn but at his side. Cara giggled.

"Dear, we don't all seem to be standing at the moment." Grettel tried to look stern, but there was a smile lurking around her lips.

"Sorry 'bout that. Don't like people assuming I can't take care of myself." Rory glanced back at Mason. He looked at the gun and another smile broke out. "This is going to be great fun." Rubbing his hands together, he hopped down from the chair and peered down at a stunned Jonathan. "Mind if I ask you some questions?" Before Jonathan could answer, or get up, Rory launched into his inquiries. Grettel produced a notebook from her bag and began to take notes.

Mason put his gun away and pulled Cara and Beth to the side. He stared at Beth for a moment, arms crossed and then spoke to Cara. "She did that on purpose."

"No," Beth said as she swallowed a laugh. "I couldn't tell."

"How many more?"

"More what?" asked Cara.

"Anything. I have heard of vampires, gargoyles, and gremlins. I have never heard of a Treshcan. So please, how many more creatures can I expect?"

"More than I have time to tell you about." Beth squeezed his arm and winked at Cara. "But I don't think there will be any more today."

"But you can't guarantee, right?"

"No, actually I can't."

"Okay, just give me a run down on them." Mason jerked his head toward the couple grilling Jonathan.

"Treshcans are the oldest Otherkin, besides vampires, that we know of. Well, we suspect there are some Bramilias left, but no one has seen them for a thousand years." At Mason's pained expression she continued quickly. "Simply put, they are magical creatures. They have incredible power but are typically gentle. They are scholarly and have kept records of everything. They are essentially explorers and researchers of every realm."

"Yeah, that's simple."

CHAPTER 48

Throughout the late afternoon Beth and Grettel went over translations in the library. Rory ran out every so often; once to ask Jonathan if he could demonstrate his speed, the second time to ask if Jonathan would mind being cut so that he could time how fast Jonathan healed. This time before Jonathan could recover enough to react, Grettel appeared and dragged Rory back to the library. Other than the Treshcans providing distraction, the day passed without incident and the team seemed to be running on an endless supply of energy.

Beth walked out of the library looking ill.

"What did they make you do?" Mason asked before realizing Beth was really upset.

"Beth?" Jonathan walked to her.

"The book might be enough," she said.

"What?" Jonathan whispered as Mason felt the tension in the room escalating.

"Christian won't be able to access all of the ancients' power, but the book might give him enough to make all the vampires he wants."

"Shit." Mason ran a hand through his hair. "How do we get it away from him if we can't fucking find him?"

"He'll find us. He still thinks he needs the Elder ring," said Jonathan.

Mason knew he was right. The tension in the room was broken when Rory poked his head out the door. Mason moved to flee, but Jonathan's speed left him in the dust. Scowling at the blur Jonathan left behind, Mason went to see what Rory wanted. He returned a short while later.

Rory had discovered that Mason was a grounder. Jonathan had given Mason up when Rory started asking rather personal questions about his libido. Jonathan casually mentioned that Mason was new to grounding. Rory had immediately cornered Mason, giving him detailed instruction on his ability. Rory was a supporter of experimentation. He'd been treating Mason like a lab rat for the last few hours of the day.

"If that Rory comes at me again I am going to shoot him." Mason sat, mentally exhausted, on the couch beside Beth.

"Won't work," Beth said.

"Will it slow him down?" Mason asked hopefully. Beth smiled and shook her head. Mason whimpered. Sheena echoed him. Rory had spent an hour trying to get her to fetch.

"Well, I think we've had a very productive day." Rory came out of the library with Grettel in tow. "Can't say when I've enjoyed myself more. You've got a nice little group here, Beth."

"Thank you, Rory."

"Well, Grettel and I will be heading to the hotel, and we'll see you bright and early in the morning. Now, you want to see something really wonderful? Watch this. Grettel, my dear." Rory took Grettel by the hand. They stood together and the air around them shimmered. As everyone watched, Rory and Grettel transformed. Their images stretched and reshaped until they stood before the gaping group looking like they had just stepped off the cover of a fashion magazine. The tone of their skin had changed to a golden tan.

"Have to blend, you know," Rory smiled broadly at them.

"You don't blend. You look like a Hollywood couple." Mason stared at Grettel, giving her a thorough once over.

"Might as well have some fun. Watch those eyes, Mason. I don't share." Rory put a possessive arm around Grettel's shoulders. "Time to go, dear, before I have to hurt one of our new friends." Grettel's laugh followed them out the door.

"That was cool," Mason said.

"Yeah, I'd like to be able to transform a few things myself," Beth said wistfully.

"You have a very nice body, Beth." Mason, Beth and Cara all turned at Jonathan's comment. "I mean—" Jonathan stammered and looked hunted. "I have to go to the office." He turned and left the room.

Cara followed him into the bedroom.

"I just meant that she shouldn't change anything. She looks good the way she is. I'm going to stop talking now." Jonathan stuttered into silence.

"It's okay. You're allowed to think Beth's pretty. I thought it was nice what you said to her." She watched him change to a suit. "I want to go with you. I know I'm needed here, in case, but I still want to go. What if he's waiting for you?"

"Can't hide forever." Jonathan dropped a kiss on her forehead.

"Be careful and hurry back." She rose to her tiptoes and kissed him good-bye.

Half an hour after Jonathan left, the phone rang. Beth answered and handed it to Cara.

"Is it Jonathan?"

"I'm not sure, but I don't think so. He sounds upset whoever he is."

"This is Cara."

"Cara?" The response on the other end was tentative.

"Who is—Danny?" *Can't possibly be!* Cara's hand tightened on the receiver. Mason hovered nearby.

"I don't know what's going on, Cara." The voice sounded lost, confused, but very much like her former partner. Unmistakably so.

"Danny?" Cara's mind couldn't wrap around the fact that it was him.

"God, I hurt so badly, I can't think straight. It took me hours to remember Beth's number."

"Who is this?" *There's no way. These last few days have been weird, but this? No way.*

"Cara? It's me. It's Danny. Honest." His voice shook. He sounded groggy, but it did sound like Danny.

"It can't be," Cara's voice firmed.

"What? Why?" Confusion and hurt came over the line.

"Because Danny's dead."

"No, no, I'm not dead. I had a nightmare I was dead. But it was a nightmare. Cara, you have to help me. I don't know what's going on. I went to my apartment and I couldn't get in. I'm a mess and I didn't want to go to the station. I need you. Cara, please."

"Prove it."

The desperation in his voice vibrated in her heart. "Prove what?"

"That you are who you say you are."

"What? What do you want to know? Listen, I can barely think straight, Cara."

"Our last shift on patrol. What did we talk about?"

"Oh, God! Cara, please. Okay, okay, give me a minute." There was silence and Cara could hear the labored breathing. "Damn! It's all fuzzy."

"Times up—"

"Wait, wait! The list! I told you I needed an assistant." His voice was frantic.

"Danny? Oh my God." Cara closed her eyes. "Where are you?" Control snapped back and Cara got Danny's location.

"Was it him?" Mason sounded unsure.

"Yes. I don't know how, but it was him. At least it was his voice and his memory." Cara began putting her new shoulder holster on. Then she slid both guns in and grabbed her extra clips. Mason followed suit.

"Let me call Jonathan before we go." Cara dialed Jonathan's cell phone but only got his voice mail. She left a message to call Beth's immediately. "Shit! Shit! Shit!" She slammed the phone down. "It's gonna get ugly. Come on, it's time to go to work."

Cara walked to the door after hugging Beth, and Mason moved to follow but Beth held him back for a moment. "Close your eyes." Beth leaned into him.

"Why?" Mason asked suspiciously.

"Trust me."

Mason closed his eyes. Cara watched as light drifted around his head and then returned to normal. "What was that?" He opened his eyes.

"It's a surprise. It will be there when you need it." Beth pulled him down and kissed his cheek.

He sprung off the step and he and Cara headed for the car. He thought for a moment, then figured Beth probably gave him some spell to help his energy.

Beth closed the door. She felt the shields fade as Cara and Mason drove away. Her strength waned, and she lay down on the couch, suddenly exhausted. Sheena padded over, laid her head on Beth's stomach, and whined.

"It's okay. They'll make it back in time." Beth put a reassuring hand on Sheena's head. Then her eyes drifted shut.

Sheena nudged her hand; the last thing Beth felt was her hand limply slide off the wolf's questioning head to the floor below.

CHAPTER 49

Cara and Mason pulled up in front of the 7-Eleven that Danny had called from. Danny limped toward the car. He was still dressed in the uniform he had been buried in, but it was torn and dirty. His eyes darted back and forth, and he appeared to be shivering even though it was ninety-five degrees outside. He slid into the back seat and rested his head.

"Thank God."

Cara saw that Mason had one pistol shoved roughly into his sock where his good right hand could snatch it at a second's notice.

"Are you all right?" Cara wanted to reach out and touch him to make sure he was real, but she didn't want to startle him. She also still had certain reservations about his coming back from the dead.

"Yes, I just want to get out of here."

Cara turned around and pulled out of the parking lot. Mason eyed Danny for a moment, then faced forward.

"We'll go to Beth's, where you can rest," Cara said.

"No need." The trembling uncertainty left Danny's voice. "We'll go where I tell you."

"What?" Cara turned in time to see Danny pull out a gun and hold it to Mason's head.

"Danny? What are you doing? Put that away."

"I don't take orders from you."

"Let me guess?" Mason said dryly. "Christian's pulling your strings."

"Better than the bitch driving," Danny snorted.

"Don't let him do this to you," insisted Cara.

"I was your lap dog. I would have done anything for you. But you never looked at me, not really. Now I hear you're fucking some vampire."

"Not to interrupt, but that *was* after you had your throat slit," Mason chimed in. Cara couldn't hold it against him. His previously normal life had taken a permanent trip down twilight road, he might as well go with it.

"Oh, yeah, super cop. What I wouldn't have given to see your face when you opened that closet door. Mr. Justice got screwed, huh?"

"You came back with a huge attitude problem, buddy. What I can't understand is how you could throw in with Christian."

"Turn right here. And keep both hands on the wheel."

Cara had no intention of making a break for it. She was going right where she wanted to be.

"Mason, old buddy, it's a funny thing, but I can't think of anything I'd rather do than serve my Savior."

Cara and Mason glanced at each other. Cara thought back to what Jonathan said about Christian making slaves. Danny continued to give directions. They ended up at the house where the four officers had been killed. Danny followed them up to the door but didn't bother to disarm them. They walked in and faced Christian, two vampires they hadn't seen before, and Cavannah.

"Ah, our final guests." Christian draped an arm around Cavannah. She didn't look happy about it, but didn't move it away either. The book lay open on a stand in front of them. Christian smiled at Danny. "You've done well, Danny. I'm pleased."

"Thank you," Danny beamed and gave a half bow.

"Oh, please," Mason rolled his eyes.

Christian's smile faded.

"I have no use for you, mortal. Your only value to me is leverage against Cara. Give me no trouble and I'll let you go."

"Fuck you." Mason smiled when he said it, drew his gun, and blew one of the nameless vamp's kneecaps out.

Christian disarmed him in a flash and slammed him against the wall. He managed to stay conscious. Christian took Cara's guns and tossed all of them in the corner. Stepping over the injured vamp, he walked to Cavannah and stroked her cheek.

"I hope you won't fail me this time."

"I won't!" Cavannah's voice was strong, but fear leaked out of her and Cara felt it.

"She's scared, Cara. I know you can feel it. It's delicious, isn't it?"

"No."

"Come now. We're all friends here." Christian moved to Cara and framed her face in his hands. "Doesn't it turn you on?"

"No, but you are making me want to vomit. Close enough?" Cara blanked her face and blacked out all emotion.

"So determined not give me anything. I was going to save you for myself. A pet. I've never had one, but it isn't to be. You kept the Elder Ring from me and now I'll have to use your power to access the book. I'll have all of it before this is over. Cavannah is going to give me your power. I wish we had time for other, more amorous pursuits, but we must proceed."

"You can't take anything from me."

"Oh, I know, it must be given freely. But I think you'll give me what I want." Christian motioned his hand toward his henchman. They flanked Mason, one a bit more slowly than the other; he still hadn't healed completely.

"Gentlemen." Christian raised his voice, as if in invitation for something.

Cara didn't have long to wait. Jonathan was dragged in between two more vamps. Vinton brought up the rear. Jonathan's body was marked with bullets and his hands and feet were bound with silver chains. They left his wrists and ankles bloody and didn't allow them to heal. They threw him to the floor.

It took everything she had, but she didn't move to Jonathan.

"I have you to thank for the silver bullets. I didn't even think of it until you slaughtered my men with them. Give me what I want, and I'll let your men go."

"I've seen this movie, Christian. Nobody gets away."

"I give you my word."

"Your word is shit!" Jonathan croaked from the floor.

"Shut up." Christian kicked Jonathan in the side.

"Let them go now, and you can have whatever you want," Cara stated unemotionally.

"No!" Jonathan and Mason echoed each other.

"Give me what I want, and then I'll let them go."

"Cara." Jonathan raised his head to look at her. Cara stared at him. While she was distracted, Christian retrieved one of the guns.

"Give me everything, Cara. Everything you are." Christian shot Jonathan in the thigh.

Cara watched. She looked back at Mason and gave him a weak smile.

Panic spread across his face. "Cara! Don't do it!" he yelled.

"You can have everything I am." She looked Christian dead in the eye.

Jonathan and Mason started to yell and struggle in earnest.

Mason's guards beat him. Danny and Vinton joined in. They weren't needed, but they looked like they were enjoying themselves.

Christian fired into Jonathan's body. Blood began to run freely, but he continued to try to escape the manacles.

"Stop it!" Cara shouted. "The deal's off if you hurt them."

"Too late," Christian smiled. Cara noticed that Cavannah had begun speaking softly, intently.

Cara took a step back.

"You're not going anywhere." Christian tossed the gun onto the floor with the others. Grabbing Cara, he pressed his lips to hers. Cavannah walked to them, continuing her whispers. She placed her hands on the back of Christian's and Cara's heads. Cara struggled, but Christian held her in place easily with one hand while his other hand ran over her body.

Jonathan and Mason were subdued and made to watch. Cara felt as if the life was being sucked out of her. Pain seared her body. Something was inside of her and it was trying to claw its way out. She wrenched her mouth away and screamed.

"Nooo!" Jonathan watched Christian release Cara. She slid to the floor. He couldn't tell if she was alive. He couldn't feel her anymore.

"Oh, Jonathan. You always did have the best taste. Or was it that your women taste best?" Christian laughed. It was almost a giggle. He stumbled back and slumped against the wall, as if the transference had sapped him of all his energy. "It's the most incredible feeling, being inside Cara. You were inside her, and now I'm inside her. She loves you. And the only lips you'll ever hear it from are mine." Christian started laughing, then slid down the wall to a sitting position. Standing looked as though it had become too much.

Cavannah continued to murmur reading from the book but the pages began to turn quickly and she looked surprised as the door to the front of the house smashed open and a huge version of Rory stepped through followed by the miniature Grettel.

"Well, boys, what's all this?"

Christian tried to stand. "Take them!" he shouted. He stood, but was wobbly. "Finish it!" Cavannah shrank back, but turned to the book. She grabbed it, and looked like she was trying to return it to the correct page, but as soon as her hands touched it she screamed. She threw the book to the floor and stared at her smoking hands in disbelief.

Jonathan watched as the guards once covering Mason rushed Rory. He fought them, and Mason grabbed the gun still stuck in his right sock. His first shot caught Vinton full in the face: it exploded in a rush of bloody pieces. Christian apparently hadn't fulfilled his promise because Vinton didn't move. He stayed dead. He took a shot at Cavannah, but she shielded herself, and the bullet's path slid to the side.

Tiny Grettel slid over to Jonathan where he lay on the floor. His two guards tried to stop the diminutive woman, but she was lightning fast and broke the manacle with her bare hands in milliseconds. Jonathan rose shakily and went after Christian across the room.

Mason stood, gauging his best bet. His hands began to tingle. Cavannah stopped and stared at him. Gaped at him. Mason dropped the gun and waited, somehow instinctively knowing that something else was coming next. The warmth from Beth returned in a hot rush and burst out of him, hitting Cavannah full force and throwing her against the wall. Her eyes fluttered shut. Mason's hands still tingled. Power flowed through him. He ran to Cara and stared down at her.

"Hold on to her, boy!" Rory shouted from the melee. "Hold onto her or you'll lose her."

Mason put his hands on her midsection. He didn't know how, but he knew she wasn't there. "She's gone!"

"She's here, I know it!" Rory fought a vamp while giving instructions to Mason.

Mason closed his eyes and concentrated, then he felt her! She was close by, hovering just above her body. He felt the energy inside him swirl around the essence that was Cara and pull her back into her body.

He drew away, then felt her being pulled from herself and repeated the process.

"I can't hold her." His whole body was thrumming with tension.

"The spell's almost complete; you have to hold her there until Christian is dead." Rory was knocked to the ground. "Why, you little bastard, I'll teach you!" He rose and grabbed the vamp's head, efficiently ripping it off his shoulders and tossing it into the corner. One of the vamps picked up a discarded weapon and shot Rory who went down. Grettel ran to him.

Christian crawled to his feet and retreated from Jonathan as he was freed. Jonathan caught up with him. Christian was weak from the exchange but managed to protect his vital areas. Quickly regaining strength, Jonathan picked Christian up and threw him into the wall. Then grabbing Mason's discarded weapons, he fired…guns…into Christian's chest. Blood sprayed. Christian's survival instinct kicked in and he flew at Jonathan. They rolled to the floor, their speed making it impossible for Mason to follow the movement. As they rolled, blood trailed them. They must have both heard Rory declare that Christian had to die in order for Cara's spirit to remain in her body, because they redoubled their efforts to kill and survive. At last Jonathan pinned Christian to the ground. He strained for release, but Jonathan held firm.

"It ends here and now." Jonathan plunged his hand into Christian's chest and grabbed his heart with his right hand.

Christian screamed and his back bowed. Jonathan squeezed and ripped with all his vampire strength. Christian's heart came out with a wet, sucking sound. Jonathan held it in front of Christian's eyes, then crushed it with one final triumphant squeeze. With a look of utter amazement on his twisted face, Christian died.

CHAPTER 50

Silence. Danny slumped on the ground. His only connection with this world was obviously Christian. Rory and Grettel had finished the other vamps; Rory kept looking about, as if hoping for another dozen or so to show up so he could continue his romp.

Mason still had his hands pressed against Cara. He felt her there, but his lack of confidence in his ability made him afraid to let go. Cara gasped. She opened her eyes slowly and blinked.

"Damn, Mason. You're good," she said weakly as he took her in his arms and lifted her to a sitting position.

"I didn't think I could hold you."

Jonathan crawled to them. Mason let her go, and she buried her head in Jonathan's shoulder as Rory and Grettel returned to their normal size.

"I haven't had that much fun in ages!" Rory couldn't stand still. Despite his wound he paced back and forth. He looked at Cavannah who was still unconscious and then he turned to Mason. "By the way, you reek of Beth's power. I don't have to hurt you, too. Do I?"

"What do you mean?"

"I know Beth's power. How did you get it?"

"She gave it to me, I guess. She did something right before I left. Said it would be there when I needed it."

"Good Lord! You have to give it back."

"What are you talking about?" Mason's head was pounding.

"She'll die, boy," Rory said quietly. "She must have her power back, or she will be no more."

"Let's go!" Mason shouted as Jonathan helped Cara to her feet.

As they headed for the door, a bright white light blocked their path. Mason made out a vaguely human shape.

"Jonathan." The voice was soft, a whisper.

"Oh, what now!" Mason yelled in frustration.

"The old ones," Rory said. "Jonathan has killed one of his own kind."

Mason and Cara moved in between Jonathan and the light.

"You cannot protect him. He must pay." The voice sounded almost amused.

"You can't do this." Cara's voice held desperation. "He did what you wanted him to do!"

"Child, it must be." A flash burst from the light, darting between Cara and Mason, hitting Jonathan square in the chest and knocking him to the floor.

"Jonathan!" Cara fell beside him.

"It's okay. Get to Beth." He seemed to have difficulty speaking. "I love you." His eyes closed.

Cara stared stunned. Mason watched as she swung around in rage but the light was gone.

"Cara, he's still breathing." Mason had a hand on his chest. "He's still there."

They carried Jonathan to the car and raced to Beth's.

Mason approached the house first. The front door stood open. He pulled out his weapon. Looking at the sky he knew he had to get Jonathan into the house quickly; the night was fading. Cara took a position on the opposite side of the door and Mason entered first.

Beth lay on the couch. A man knelt on the floor, bending over her.

"Get up. Slowly," Mason commanded.

The man started and rose. He was six foot five if he was an inch. Well muscled but not bound by it. His head was completely bald, but his face had a mustache and goatee. Black suede vest, snug black jeans, and black boots with silver tips made up his clothes. His sapphire blue eyes stared steadily at Mason.

"She's dying."

"Get away from her."

He moved to the side. Cara trained her gun on him while Mason checked Beth.

"What's going on, Cara?" the man asked.

"Do I know you?" Cara studied him. He looked like a biker from *GQ*.

"It's Thomas," he smiled.

Mason thought of Danny. "How can we be sure?"

"Sheena knows it's me." He nodded to the wolf who trotted to his side and Cara lowered her gun.

"Who's that?" Thomas put his hands down and motioned behind her.

"Rory. I'll explain later. Right now we need to save Beth."

"Mason," Rory moved to the couch where Beth lay. "Do what you did for Cara. This time take what's inside of you and put it back into her."

Mason felt uncertain but placed his hands on Beth. He searched inside for that power, the energy that Beth had given him. Surprised at how easily he found it, he pushed it into Beth. He felt it leave and enter her and then he looked at Rory for a cue.

"You can let go now. Son, you're getting to be quite good at this sort of thing, a natural I would say." Rory moved Mason to the side and checked Beth. "She'll sleep for a while yet, but she should be fine. I do believe you made it in time," he added reassuringly.

"Should be? Believe?"

"There are never any guarantees in life, my boy. Now let's get your friend inside, the sun is coming."

"Jonathan?" Thomas asked as though he had assumed him dead.

"He killed Christian," Mason informed him.

"What happened to him?" Thomas asked as he made for the car.

"We don't know yet."

CHAPTER 51

Jonathan remained unconscious. No movement, nothing, for a solid week. They took turns in his room watching him. Introductions were made, explanations given. They discovered that Cavannah was being held by the Governors.

Beth had screamed bloody murder when she woke to find the giant Thomas standing over her, next to her bed. She calmed down once she realized who it was, but she scared the shit out of him.

The Treshcans were making headway translating the book, but nothing of any help had been found yet.

Mason had apologized to Thomas for getting him killed. Several times in fact. Thomas finally told him to shut up.

Mason wandered into the library.

"Hello, my boy," said Rory. "Cara told me you had both decided to leave the police. Are you sure that's what you want?"

"I can't see going back. There are too many things I can't explain to them. No reasonable explanations I can give."

"True. What will you do now?"

"I'm throwing around a couple of ideas. You know, I was wondering, Beth said you guys were supposed to be scholarly and gentle. You weren't particularly gentle last week. That was pretty incredible watching you tear a vampire's head right from his shoulders." Mason took a seat beside Rory.

"As a general rule we are, but we could not sit by and watch our friends die."

"How'd you know where we were?"

"I called Beth's, and no one answered. Grettel and I followed the energy, so to speak."

"Why couldn't we do that to locate Christian?"

"Low energy. Hard to detect. But with all of you there, the energy poured over the whole area."

"That's the simplest answer I've heard in the last three weeks."

"Glad to be of help. Now I have a few questions."

"Oops, look at the time. I have to go relieve Thomas." Mason fled the library. He set himself up in the chair in Jonathan's room. He'd taken to studying his ability while he sat with Jonathan. An hour into his book, he thought he caught a movement. He looked up. There, he did move. His hand twitched. Mason moved toward the bed. Jonathan blinked and Mason's jaw dropped.

He turned to get the others, but Jonathan caught his wrist. It was incredibly strong for someone who had lain in bed for a week.

"I'm hungry," Jonathan rasped.

"Oh, shit." Mason swallowed hard. "Guys!" He yelled for the others. People came from everywhere.

"Oh my God!" Cara was the first to get there.

"He's hungry. Tell him I'm not dinner." Mason tugged on his arm and Jonathan let go.

Cara approached the bed.

"Not like that." Jonathan cleared his throat. "I want food."

"What?" Cara looked confused.

"Food. A steak, an apple, potato chips. Food."

Cara still looked perplexed but went into the kitchen and made a sandwich quickly.

Mason helped Jonathan sit up. He inhaled the sandwich.

"Thirsty," Jonathan said around his last bite of sandwich.

"I'm gone," Mason moved to leave.

"Stupid… Water. No, wait, get me one of those things Beth is always drinking, Diet Coke."

Mason went to get it. Jonathan drank the whole thing without a pause. They sat around the bed and stared at him.

"What's going on?" Jonathan looked at them.

"You got me," Mason shrugged.

Jonathan glanced over Mason's shoulder at the bald man.

"Thomas?"

"Yeah," Thomas stared at him curiously.

They moved Jonathan to the living room. He ate a baked potato, a salad, bread, cheese, and had two more Diet Cokes. The new pastime seemed to have shifted to watching him eat.

"Not that I don't appreciate that attention but—"

"I've got it!" Rory jumped up from the chair and moved to within inches of Jonathan's face. "You're human."

"Come again?"

"Human," Rory looked around the room for confirmation.

"That's the big punishment?" Jonathan didn't look as though he believed him.

Rory reasoned, "Why did all these rules get put into place to begin with? Because, certain factions of vampires turned on the humans. They considered mortals to be beneath them; they hated feeling as if they served them. What better way to punish someone than to turn him into what they hated?" Rory looked smug.

"Human." Jonathan shook his head. "It's so simple."

"But he's still strong," Mason threw out.

"We'll have to run tests to see how much of your abilities you retained. Over a period of time, of course, because we want to make sure they are permanent." Rory walked away, muttering to himself about timetables and tests.

"Do you think I can still move fast enough to outrun him?" Jonathan rubbed his hands over his face. He turned to Cara. "What does this mean for us?"

"I can get used to it."

Jonathan pulled her down to him. Feeling awkward, Mason snuck out of the room.

Beth caught Thomas in the kitchen. She stared at his new body.

"I know it's hard to get used to. It's hard for me to adjust." He was fidgeting. Thomas looked away as though he were embarrassed to meet her eyes.

She pulled a chair up next to him and climbed on top of it so they were face to face. She tenderly turned his head to her, and they locked eyes. "I know how to lift the curse."

ABOUT THE AUTHOR

When she's not dreaming of other worlds, Traci Houston lives in Southbury, Connecticut, with her husband and two children. Please look for more tales of The Otherkin coming out soon.